The Secret Of Kells

THE NOVEL

EITHNE MASSEY is a graduate of University College Dublin and NUI Maynooth, and a short-story writer. She has worked with the Arts Council and as a librarian. Her interest in mythology has been a lifelong one.

Eithne lives between Ireland and a cottage in Brittany, which is surrounded by oak forests very like those in *The Secret of Kells*. No wolves have been spotted, but there are wild boar, foxes, deer, fire salamanders, squirrels and many birds.

In the novelisation of the movie, *The Secret of Kells*, Eithne brings to life the story of the orphaned Brendan, from the monastery of Kells and his part in the completion of one of the world's most famous and treasured books, the Book of Kells.

Eithne is also the author of *Blood Brother, Swan Sister, Where the Stones Sing, The Silver Stag of Bunratty, The Dreaming Tree* and *Best-Loved Irish Legends*.

THE NOVEL

eithne massey

illustrated by the cartoon saloon

based on the film the secret of kells

written by tomm moore and fabrice ziolkowski

THE O'BRIEN PRESS
DUBLIN

First published 2009 by The O'Brien Press Ltd.
12 Terenure Road East, Rathgar, Dublin 6, Ireland.
Tel: +353 1 4923333; Fax: +353 1 4922777
E-mail: books@obrien.ie; Website: www.obrien.ie
Reprinted 2009, 2011, 2012, 2015.

ISBN 978-1-84717-121-4

10 9 8 7 6 5
19 18 17 16 15

Editing, typesetting and design: The O'Brien Press Ltd.

Printing: Nørhaven, Denmark

The paper used in this book is produced using pulp from managed forests.

The O'Brien Press receives assistance from

contents

prologue

*L*ong ago, in an Ireland of huge forests, there were no towns, only small settlements. Some of these settlements had an abbey where monks gave their lives to God and to the creation of the most beautiful books in the world.

One such place was called Kells, the home of a boy called Brendan. This is Brendan's story, a story of the terrors of the dark forests, the raiders from the northern seas and a fabulous, timeless treasure.

1 The cat and the tower

Brendan held his breath. He didn't dare make a sound, didn't dare move, trapped as he was in the little passage beneath the Abbot's cell. Through the gap in the stones he could see the two figures; one very tall, wearing a dark red cloak; the other smaller and white haired. The tall figure was his uncle, the Abbot of Kells, the smaller one was a new arrival to the monastery, Brother Aidan of Iona. Aidan was the owner of the white cat who was digging her claws into his chest. Brendan was terrified that she would make a noise. If she did, he would be discovered by his uncle. Then there would be trouble. He was in enough trouble already. He was always in trouble with his uncle, the Abbot.

And it was not really his fault. Brendan had not

meant to eavesdrop. It had all been because of the cat, Pangur Bán. She had not been pleased at being left in his charge and had run away from him. So he had had to follow her, all the way up the stairs of the Abbot's tower. He had almost caught her when she had disappeared through a gap in the great blocks of stone. He had wriggled in after her and so had found his way into the little passage-way hidden beneath the floor. Now Pangur looked at him, in a superior catlike way, as he held her tight, afraid to breathe in case the two monks heard him.

At least his uncle had his back to him. He was standing in front of the wall where his great plan was drawn, the plan for the defence of Kells. Every detail of the monastery had been carefully filled in. Abbot Cellach had a ruler in his hand and was pointing out the different parts of the drawing.

'This circle,' he said, giving a wide sweep of the ruler, 'is the enclosure of the monastery. All the wooden fences are being replaced by a stone wall. As you can imagine, it is a huge job.' He sighed, and Brendan knew he was thinking of all the work still to be done. Then he continued, 'In the centre is the Church. It is dedicated to St Colmcille. And beside it here is the Round Tower.'

Now he was smiling. 'I don't think you have those in Scotland. It's a new idea, building them. The Tower is an excellent refuge from attack. It stands over eighty-eight feet high, and has only one door, about six and a half feet up the wall. The look-out windows face out in five directions. That's my idea; there are usually only four, but five gives a much broader view. It means we will have good warning of when the enemy attacks. If there is an attack, we can bring the villagers in here and take refuge, pulling up the ladder. And here you can see the monks' huts, the Dining-Hall, the Guest House and of course the Scriptorium.'

Aidan interrupted, 'Ah, the Scriptorium, where the books are made. That is what I wanted to talk to you about ...'

The Abbot looked annoyed. He hated to be interrupted in the middle of his lecture. Brendan knew the lecture by heart. He had heard it so many times that he usually didn't listen any more.

The Abbot said abruptly, 'We don't have time at the moment to be making books. Building the walls is the important work now. The walls will protect all of us from the attacks of the Northmen. And it will protect the refugees that come to us now; the pagans and Crom worshippers. Through the strength of our walls they will come to trust the strength of our faith.'

Now the Abbot was pointing out the various weak points in the wall that needed work, explaining his plan to his companion. It seemed to Brendan that Brother Aidan was not really interested in the wall.

'Brother Cellach,' he said, 'you must know that all the walls in the world will not be able to keep them out. Nothing can stop them. There are too many of them. Our work should be to make something that will outlast us, something that will still be there when all the walls are down, and all of us long gone. That will turn the darkness into light. That is why the Book is so important.'

'I don't want to hear about the Book!' The Abbot spoke quietly. Brendan's uncle never raised his voice. He never had to. All he had to do was give you a look from his steely grey eyes, and you immediately did just what you had been told to do.

Brendan's problem was that he so often forgot what it was that he had been told to do. He would happily begin to do the task he had been set. But then his attention would be caught by something: the way a spider spun its web in the sunlight, a beetle carrying a crumb home to its family or the call of a cuckoo coming from the forest beyond the walls of the monastery ...

That was what had happened that morning. He had been on his way to the Scriptorium to collect some plans for the Abbot. All of a sudden, he had heard a great fuss behind him and he had been nearly knocked over by a large goose flying past. Brother Leonardo was hot on its heels. The goose was honking madly, and Brother Leonardo had honked too, 'Catch her, Brendan!' He had called as he ran: 'Don't let her get away!'

As the chase continued, half the monks in the monastery, glad of an excuse to stop lifting stones for the wall, had joined Brendan and Leonardo.

Finally, after Brother Leonardo had fallen in the pigpen and the goose had disrupted a game of hurling, they had caught her, all of them falling over with laughter ... and taken five of her tail feathers to use as pens in the Scriptorium. But this escapade had meant that Brendan had been late bringing the plans to his uncle, who had not been at all pleased.

'Brendan,' Abbot Cellach had said, 'how am I to trust you with responsibility when you continue to disappoint me? One day you will take control of this abbey, yet it takes you several hours to fulfil a simple task. What will happen when you have to take on responsibility for Kells? Responsibility for all the brothers and all the villagers and all the people who have come to us, begging us to keep them safe behind these walls? You must learn to concentrate!'

Luckily, this particular lecture – which Brendan also knew by heart – had been interrupted by the arrival of Brother Aidan at the gates of the monastery. Brother Aidan, who had come all the way from Iona, far across the sea.

What Brendan needed to concentrate on at the moment was not sneezing. The smell of old damp stone was catching in his throat. He shut his eyes tight and just about managed to keep the sneeze in. The cat was staring into Brendan's eyes. She was a strange creature. Her own eyes were odd coloured, one blue, one green. Aidan was still trying to argue with Abbot Cellach.

'Ah, but if you would only take a look at the Book, Cellach. It is a masterpiece, as fine as anything ever created on Iona, even by Colmcille himself. Indeed, it was Colmcille who began it. It was put into my keeping when Iona was destroyed and I promised to bring it here, to your monastery where it would be safe.'

The Abbot, as always, was not listening. Now he continued, 'You are not the first refugee from the Northmen that we have had here, Aidan. And you will not be the last. There are streams of people seeking refuge, new ones almost every week. That means that the enemy is coming closer to this place every day. They have burned Rathlin and Lambay and many others. They have stolen the treasures, the gold and the jewels. They have killed and wounded all who cross their path. And then they take their great boats and go back across the sea with our treasures and our cattle and our children, our children, Aidan, made into slaves. And they sit quiet for a while and plan the next bloody raid on our peaceful island. I know my duty. It is to look after those who seek refuge in this monastery from the slaughterers, from the curse of the Northmen – not to make books, no matter how beautiful.'

Aidan quietly interrupted him. His voice was very sad when he spoke. 'I know all too well what the Northmen do when they attack, Cellach. I was in Iona when they arrived. I saw my brothers' blood stain the grey rocks red. There was nothing left when they had finished with us but a smoking ruin and the smell of death, and the black crows coming down from the skies ... I was lucky that I had a hiding place, and legs that would carry me away. And something was saved from all the horror. Look ...'

He picked up the worn leather satchel that he kept close by him.

'Let me show you the Book ...'

Cellach interrupted him again, 'If you have seen all those terrible things, I do not know why you cannot see why we need this wall!'

'And I do not know why you cannot see how we need the Book ...' Aidan spoke quietly, and turned to leave the Abbot's cell. But then he stopped, and looked down. Brendan's heart almost stopped too. Had he seen Brendan and Pangur?

'Abbot Cellach,' he said, turning back, 'one last thing. Tell me about the boy, Brendan. He's your sister's child, isn't he? He has a real look of her.'

'Yes, he's my poor sister's child alright. I found him after the Northmen had come down the river and attacked his people. He was only a tiny baby. I took him up, wrapped him in my cloak and brought him here. He has been here since. He knows of no world apart from the monastery.'

'It's a sad story. I'm sorry to hear it,' said Aidan. He paused. 'But he seems a good lad.'

The Abbot snorted. 'He's a good lad when he keeps his mind on things, which isn't as often as it

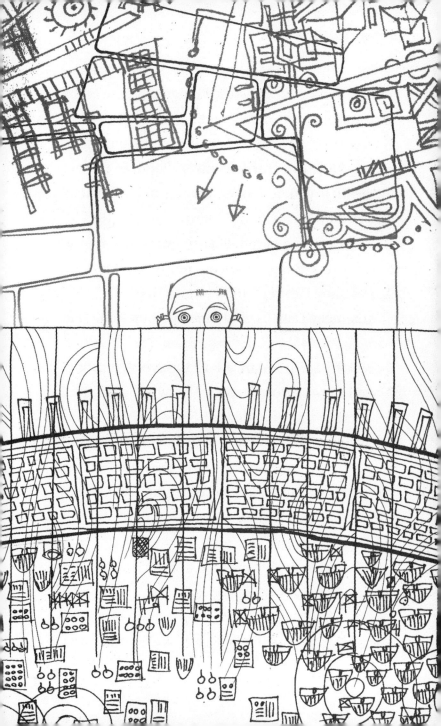

should be. He likes to spend too much time in the Scriptorium.'

'You used to love to spend time in the Scriptorium too. You were no mean hand at the old illustration yourself, once upon a time, Cellach,' said Aidan.

Cellach's face became hard again. 'I have no time for such things now. And nor has anyone else in this monastery.'

'You mean there is only time for your wall,' said Aidan.

'Not my wall, Aidan, a wall to save civilisation! A wall to save your book! Now we should go. I have many things to do.'

The two monks made their way to the door. But as Aidan walked past the gap in the wall Brendan was almost sure he looked down and winked at Brendan.

2 the book

The rest of the day was very busy. Brendan had a long list of chores to do. One of the Abbot's favourite sayings was: 'The devil finds work for idle hands.' So he made very sure that there were no idle hands in Kells. As well as their daily tasks in the monastery, the monks had other duties. They met at regular times in the chapel, to sing and to pray. Brendan spent many hours there, crammed in with the monks in the dark candlelit space. He quite liked the long ceremonies, so long as he didn't have to sit beside Brother Friedrich, whose feet were a bit smelly. The time in the chapel gave his mind a chance to wander wherever it chose to go. Nobody noticed, so long as he didn't forget to take part in the chanting and praying. The monks also all met at dinner, where they sat at long wooden tables in the Refectory, with the only light coming from rush-lights and the great open fires, where half-trunks of forest trees flamed brightly. Tonight, there was extra food and the Abbot sat at the top table with Aidan. For once, Abbot Cellach smiled and laughed during the meal. He seemed to be sharing jokes with Aidan, old jokes that no one else knew. Brendan tried to remember the last time he had heard the Abbot laugh, and found that he could not. Everybody ate the same simple meal: a dish of lentil soup and coarse brown bread. Very often the monks were not allowed to speak at meals, but this evening, in celebration of Aidan's arrival, the Abbot had allowed conversation. So Brendan got a chance to ask his particular friends about Aidan.

'Ah, the great Aidan!' said Brother Tang. Brother Tang was small and round and very kind. He had come to Kells from far in the east, travelling mile after mile in his search for wisdom. And he was very wise. The Abbot trusted him more than anyone else in the monastery, and sometimes even followed his advice, although as a general rule Cellach did not listen to anybody.

Now Tang sounded unusually excited about the

new arrival. 'Brother Aidan is an old friend of Abbot Cellach – they were young monks together in Clonmacnoise. Aidan is the perfect illuminator, a master, one of the most skilful of our times. His work outshines what we do in the Scriptorium here in the same way the sun outshines that rush-light on the table. We are greatly honoured to have him here among us.'

'If only Abbot Cellach would let him teach us!' said Brother Assoua. Brother Assoua was large and black. He had come to Kells from the south, from Africa. He had the best sense of humour of anybody in the monastery. He told Brendan marvellous tales of his country – about the beasts there that you could never find in Ireland: huge elephants, and monkeys that swung from the branches of trees and seemed almost human, and about the great golden lions who wandered over the sun-baked plains. Brendan particularly loved Assoua's stories about the lions.

Now, as he spoke, the rest of the monks nodded. There was Brother Friedrich, who was from the north, a Goth. He was wide as a door and as strong as an ox. He was seated beside Brother Leonardo, who was from Italy and did all the cooking in the monastery. Leonardo was a brilliant cook, even if he was a little over excitable. Next to him was Brother Jacques from France. He was the bell ringer and spent most of his time napping. Brendan had known all the monks ever since he was a baby. They were like his family, although they were all much older than he was. Like a family too, they often squabbled, especially Brother Leonardo and Brother Assoua.

Brother Assoua continued, 'You know that Aidan comes from Iona. Have you heard about Iona, Brendan?'

Brendan shook his head.

'Iona is one of the greatest monasteries in the world. It is – it was – built on a tiny island to the east and to the north of us, near Scotland. The monks thought that they were safe because they were on an island. But Northmen came by the sea and attacked it. '

'My uncle says islands are never really safe.' Brendan's voice was wistful. He knew he would never see Iona, or any other island. His uncle would never allow him to travel so far beyond the walls of the monastery. He was not even allowed to go out into the forest that surrounded Kells. Brendan knew that his uncle had made these rules to protect him, to keep him safe, as he had tried to do ever since he had saved him from the Northmen. But he still longed to see the world outside the walls of Kells.

There was a silence after Brendan spoke, and then Leonardo continued, 'But Iona was safe for a long time. The monastery had been there for over two hundred years. It was founded by the great Colmcille himself.'

'The same Colmcille our church is called after?' asked Brendan.

Brother Leonardo nodded. 'Yes, the same. Colmcille was from Donegal, from a royal family. He would have been a prince if he had not decided to become a monk. And he became one of the greatest saints and greatest abbots the world has ever known. He made the most beautiful books, over three hundred of them. You know, that was why he left Ireland in the first place, because of an argument over a book. He was a man with a terrible temper, and a great warrior. He copied a book that a monk called Finnian had illustrated, and Finnian was so angry with him they ended up fighting one another. Of course, all that was before he became a saint. Other people joined in the row so that in the end there was a huge battle. Colmcille won, but many, many people were killed. After the battle, when Colmcille saw what had happened because of his anger, he punished himself by leaving Ireland. He swore never to set foot on Irish soil again, though he loved the country with all his heart. He went across the sea to Iona. They say he started to make a book there, and that book is the most beautiful one ever created. It is called the Book of Iona and to look into it is to gaze into heaven. Sinners are blinded if they dare to look inside. No one has ever matched the way Colmcille was able to draw, the details of the designs he made. That was because ...'

Brother Leonardo stopped for a moment and then whispered, 'Colmcille was only able to draw the way he did because he had a third eye.'

'He hadn't a third eye!' interrupted Brother Assoua loudly. 'He had a third hand. And he had twelve fingers on each of them.'

The two brothers looked as if they were going to have one of their arguments, so Brendan blurted out quickly, 'Whichever he had, he must have been a strange-looking character!'

Everyone laughed.

'And what happened to all the books they illustrated on Iona after the Northmen started to come and raid the monastery?' asked Brendan.

Brother Assoua sighed. 'They must have been destroyed, lad. The Northmen have no respect for reading or the beauty of art. They are all gone, lost, like so many other treasures.'

Brendan said nothing. Because of the conversation he had overheard, he knew better. There was one book, at least, which had escaped the Northmen, and that book was in Aidan's satchel. All through dinner and all through the service in the chapel afterwards, Brendan thought about the Book. It was surely the one that Colmcille himself had begun, the most beautiful book in the world.

Brendan crept through the darkness to the Scriptorium. When he had gone to his cell, he had found that he couldn't sleep. He had tossed and turned, thinking about the Book and imagining what it would look like. He finally decided that he had to see it. He had noticed that Aidan had left the Book in the Scriptorium when they went to pray in the church. As he sneaked up the stairs, he saw that there was a glow of light coming from under the door. He opened the door very carefully in case someone was there. If it was his uncle, he would be in trouble again. But then his uncle hardly ever went to the Scriptorium. When he entered the room there was only one faintly shining rush-light left on one of the tables. But a golden glow seemed to come from the worn leather satchel that Brother Aidan had carried. Brendan crept a little closer. There was something there, a black shape against the light, but he could not make out what it was. As he groped his way through the half-darkness, it seemed to expand, growing bigger and bigger until it became huge and monstrous. The shadow of a dark, beast-like demon. A shadow which leapt for his throat and shrieked at him like a banshee!

Brendan yelled. The cat leapt on top of the satchel. Her back was arched and her fur stood on end as she hissed at him, warning him to keep away.

'You nearly killed me with fright, Pangur Bán,' whispered Brendan, taking a deep breath. 'I don't mean the Book any harm. I know you are just trying to guard it. I just want to see it. All I've ever seen is inside the walls of Kells. If I could just see one page ... please?'

The cat looked hard at Brendan. Then she seemed to make up her mind. She stopped hissing and moved down from the satchel. She seated herself nearby, looking at Brendan with what seemed almost a smile on her face. Brendan realised that Pangur had accepted him and that they had suddenly become friends.

And so, very gently, Brendan started to pull the Book from the bag. It was heavy, and he needed both hands to do it. He could feel metal and leather. But he had only pulled it out a little way when a voice behind him said, 'Well if it isn't the little brother with the big questions!'

Brendan nearly dropped the Book in fright. It was Aidan, looking rather sleepy, but not at all cross. But Brendan felt dreadful. He could feel his face go very red as he stuttered, 'I'm ... I ... I didn't mean to ...'

Aidan interrupted, 'I understand. You got bored eavesdropping on the Abbot's private conversations and decided to rummage through my things.'

Brendan was horrified. He didn't know what to say.

Aidan smiled. 'Calm down, lad, calm down. I won't tell on you.'

Brendan's face went even redder.

'I didn't mean to eavesdrop, honestly – it was Pangur that ran away and I chased her up the stairs.'

'Blaming the cat, now, is it?' said Aidan. But he smiled as he said it so Brendan knew he was only joking. The old monk continued, 'That cat, now, is a very wise cat, and might well have known what she was doing when she led you up those stairs. So, you want to see the Book? Go on then, take a look.'

Brendan looked at him. Did he mean it?

'Go on then,' Aidan said again. 'Take a look.'

But now Brendan stopped. He had just remembered something.

'The brothers say that sinners are blinded if they look at the Book ...'

Aidan's smile grew wider. 'Is that what you really believe will happen?' He paused for a moment. 'I can't tell you what will happen when you look, Brendan. It's up to you to make the choice. There's nothing in this life but mist, is there, lad? It's your decision, no one else's.'

Still Brendan hesitated. He could stop now, because he was afraid, but then he would never see the Book. And more than anything else in the world he wanted to see it.

Slowly, Brendan pulled the Book out from the satchel. He gulped when he saw the magnificent

cover. It was covered in gold and silver, and studded with jewels. Rubies and emeralds and amethysts sparkled in the light. He ran his fingers over the gold.

'The cover is not the real treasure,' said Aidan. 'Go on, open it up ...'

Very slowly, very carefully, Brendan opened the cover and looked inside.

3 into the forest

Brendan never forgot the moment when he saw the first page of the Book. It was the colours that struck him first. As he looked at the yellows and the reds, the purples and blues and greens, he felt as if he were drowning. Drowning in a sea of the most beautiful colours he had ever seen. They appeared to glow with light, to shine even more brightly than the jewels on the cover. And the more he looked, the further he was drawn into the pictures. The spiral paths led his eyes deeper and deeper into a secret space, a magic place – into a world of tiny, intricate figures and designs. The figures were of men and angels, of birds and beasts and flowers. Swirls and spirals, knotwork and mazes; each bright band of colour held a meaning and each pattern held a message. For a long time he looked into this world, slowly turning the pages as more and more marvellous things met his eyes. He was not aware of where he was, of how long he looked, but finally he croaked, his voice hardly more than a whisper, 'The work of angels.'

Aidan laughed. 'The work of angels – did you hear that, Pangur? I didn't know they made angels as funny looking as me! Maybe the boy *has* gone blind!'

Then he became serious. 'I thought the very same when I first saw it. But 'tis only the work of mere mortals, I'm afraid. Mortals like me – or you. The Book was created as a vision of beauty, a beacon in these dark days of the Northmen. And do you want to see the most beautiful page? The one that will turn darkness into light?'

Brendan nodded.

Aidan leaned over the Book, turning the pages until he came to one which he opened out.

Brendan's mouth fell open in astonishment. The page was blank.

'There now,' said Aidan. 'That's to be the Chi Ro page.'

'The what?' said Brendan. 'But there is nothing on it.'

'That's right,' said Aidan. 'The Chi Ro page has nothing on it yet, because the Book has not been finished. That page is to be the glory of the Book, the one filled with the name of the Lord. But it has still to be decorated. And that is why I came here, because I thought I would find a refuge here, where I could continue with the Book. I thought that my old friend Cellach would support me in the work. But Cellach has changed. He can think of nothing now but building walls. It seems that once he put on that Abbot's cloak, he forgot the importance of the work he once loved. And now ...' Aidan sighed, then continued, 'Tell me, Brendan, would you like to help me?'

Brendan's heart leapt with excitement. He could imagine nothing more wonderful than to be allowed help Aidan with the work on the Book.

'Oh yes, please!' he said. 'Of course I will. I often help the brothers get their quill pens from the geese, and clean up after them. And they show me things, how to make the shapes and the letters and the little figures. They let me practise with chalk or charcoal from the fire or on one of the wax tablets, like those over there on the shelf. Leonardo says I'm not bad, and he's one of the best artists in Kells.'

He stopped, realising that he was babbling with excitement. But Aidan was smiling at him.

'Calm down, little brother!' he said. 'Now, one of the first things we have to do is to make more ink. The ink here is all very well I've had a look at it but it's not up to the standard of what we used in Iona. We want this book to last, so that people will still come to see it, and read the story that's told in it, far into the future. So we can't afford to use ink that will fade over the years. We had some special ways of making ink in Iona. I'll show them to you.'

Aidan rooted in the satchel and pulled out some little brown berries.

'You see these? Don't look like much, do they?'

Brendan shook his head.

'Well, these are what we made the green ink from – the most beautiful emerald colour you'll ever see. Look ...' He pointed to a vivid green serpent coiled around the letter S on one of the pages.

'A green like that. If you help me get a dozen or so of these, I'll show you how to make the ink.'

Brendan looked closely at the page, then at the berry Aidan held out. He had never seen one like that.

'It's not even green. Where do you get it from?' he asked.

'Why, in the forest. It's an oak gall. Do you think you could get me some of these, Brendan?'

There was a silence. Brendan didn't know what to say. 'I, I ... I'm not allowed out into the forest. My uncle says it is too dangerous out there ...'

Aidan looked at him. Then he sighed and sat down at one of the desks. 'And you know what, Brendan, he is right,' he said. 'There are terrible dangers out there, beyond the walls of the monastery. And especially in the forest. Wolves and worse. But it is possible to come through them. I came through them to get here.' He paused. 'Have you never wanted to see outside, Brendan?'

Brendan thought for a moment. 'Sometimes I have. Especially when the spring is here and the leaves come on the trees and I can hear all the birds singing. It seems so lovely out there. So full of life.'

'It is lovely,' said Aidan. 'You know, there is not just danger out there. The forest can be as beautiful as heaven, Brendan. You would see miracles there. Blessed Colmcille loved the woods. He used to say he would rather suffer the torments of hell than hear the trees being cut down in his beloved oak woods in Derry. He said there was an angel in every tree. If my brothers from Iona were here now, they would tell you that you could learn more in the forest than you ever could behind these walls, Brendan.'

Aidan sighed again. 'But I do not want to force you to go outside. For, as your uncle said, it is very dangerous. I would go myself, but I am a bit old to be climbing trees. God be with the days when I could. Now, we must try to get some sleep. Good night, Brendan.'

As Pangur and Aidan left the Scriptorium, something rolled off the desk. Brendan caught it before it fell to the floor. It was a little brown berry.

Back in his cell, Brendan found that he could still

not get to sleep. His head was full of the wonderful colours of the Book. Then he thought of how dreadful it would be if it was never to be finished. He wished he could go out into the forest to find the berries that were needed to complete the Chi Ro page. He thought of how happy Aidan would be if he brought them to him. He thought of how proud he would feel to be able to help his new friend. And then he thought of his uncle, how angry and disappointed *he* would be if he found out that Brendan had disobeyed him.

Brendan thought of the forest itself, the forest that surrounded the monastery for miles and miles, the forest where he had never been, at least not so far as he could remember. Of course, he had been brought through it on his journey to the Abbey when he was a baby. His uncle had carried him through those woods, when he had brought him to Kells, and kept him safe inside the walls he had built. If Uncle Cellach had not come to get him, he would probably have died. He owed his uncle everything, so how could he risk disappointing and hurting him yet again?

But maybe he could get the berries without his uncle finding out. Perhaps he could go into the forest and be back before anyone knew he had gone. And Aidan would have the berries to make ink, and he would make the Chi Ro page, the most beautiful page of the most beautiful book in the world. Brendan would have been the one to make it possible. But how would he get out? The big wooden gates were always locked and his uncle held the keys of all the doors and gates in the Abbey of Kells. Then he remembered something.

When he had been chasing the goose earlier that day he had found himself at a part of the walls that had still not been finished. Through the grey stone and wooden scaffolding, he had seen a ray of light, a narrow green tunnel to the forest outside. The gap there was a small one, but big enough for a thin boy to creep through. If I slipped out through there, he thought, no one would know that I had even left the enclosure of Kells.

And, he thought, if I keep thinking about the Book, I won't be afraid of the dark!

There was nobody about as Brendan made his way through the silent monastery. The rooster that slept on top of the henhouse looked sleepily at him, then stuck his head back under his wing, deciding it was still too early to crow. Brendan crept along the wall, searching for the gap he had seen during the goose hunt the previous day. He reached the place where a piece of sackcloth was hanging loosely against the scaffolding and lifting it, he could see where the light came through from the other side of the wall. He gave a quick glance behind him, but he could not see anybody. He lifted the sackcloth further, so he could creep through. But just as he did, something touched his shoulder. He almost jumped out of his skin, imagining the Abbot's angry face looking down on him. Then, with a sigh of relief, he realised that it was only Pangur Bán, who had come to keep him company.

'Pangur!' he whispered. 'Thanks for coming with me!'

The two of them entered into a tunnel of green

light. He could hear his own breath in the deep silence. He wriggled his way through the dark passage in the scaffolding, Pangur following close behind. Ahead of them, he could see a patch of light and as he moved through the tunnel the light became stronger. When he came out the other side, the sun dazzled him. He could feel a breeze, blowing more wildly than any breeze he had ever felt inside the monastery. The world smelled different. This was the wide world; there were no walls to keep him safe here. He was in the forest.

When he had seen the forest from the top of the Round Tower, it had seemed like a green sea of leaves surrounding the monastery. Now he was under the waves. And it was beautiful there. Brendan could not understand why his uncle did not want him to see such a beautiful place. Green branches, covered in lichen, twined together over his head. He touched one with his hand; it felt warm and soft as Pangur's fur. Much of the floor of the forest was covered in moss, so that he felt he was walking on a green rug. Some of the trees did not yet have their leaves, and he could see the small buds on many of the branches, but even so he could feel the green life all around him. Birds began to sing, more and more of them joining in, as if overcome with excitement that the sun had actually come up *again*.

He followed what seemed to be a path, twisting through the overhanging branches of tall trees. Butterflies flew past, bright yellows and scarlets, then a dragonfly, its colour the most luminous blue. A robin chirped busily. Something moved suddenly to his right and he realised that he had almost walked into a brown deer. He had not seen it, as it had been carefully camouflaged against a tree trunk. He watched, delighted, as its white bobtail disappeared into the trees.

He heard water, and now the path crossed a clear amber stream, with an otter standing on the bank, its black button nose alert and twitching. A frog croaked from a hole in the side of an old tree, and rabbits and hares darted across his path. In a strange way, the feeling in the forest somehow reminded Brendan of the Scriptorium. It brought him back to those times when all the monks were working hard; when everyone was quiet, so concentrated and so contented in their work that it felt as if their brains were buzzing together like happy bees. Pangur darted about, playing, grabbing at butterflies with her paws, but not seriously trying to catch them. The butterflies themselves seemed to be enjoying the game, because they would dart close, as if teasing her a little.

But as he walked on, the sun went behind a cloud and a mist rose. The shadows among the trees became darker, and the path disappeared. The trees themselves became taller, and their branches seemed to have become more tangled up in one another, blocking his path. Brendan started to imagine things. Was that a nest of snakes, there to his left? No, only intertwined branches, covered in bright moss, seen from the corner of his eye. But that was surely a pair of green eyes watching through the branches? Or had it been just a trick of the light?

Now the forest no longer seemed so beautiful.

The feeling of being caught in a web became stronger, as if the net of trees might pull him down and smother him in dead leaves. He found he was walking faster. Sharp, hidden branches tripped him and pulled at his hair and clothes. Pangur no longer played, no longer ran around. She walked straight in front of him, her tail held up stiffly and the fur on the back of her neck a white ruff of fear. Brendan took her up into his arms and hugged her tight.

The forest had become very silent. The birds had stopped singing and the breeze had died down. Even the trees were not making a sound. And it had become cold. Cold and dark and frightening. There could be anything at all watching him from the shadows. Was that another pair of eyes, red this time, glinting through the darkness?

And where was he? He had wandered through the forest without really paying much attention to his path. He looked around at the trees and all of them looked the same. He realised that he was lost. There was nothing to show him what direction he had come from, or how to find his way home.

There was no sign of the Round Tower or the tall grey walls of Kells. No sign of the monastery, the monastery that no longer seemed like a prison but like a place of safety. He came to a stream – surely, the same one he had seen quite soon after he left home? Or could it be another stream entirely?

'If I follow the water, I am bound to come back to the walls, amn't I?' he said to Pangur, who was walking by his side again, not looking at all happy. She just looked back at him.

'But then if I do that, what direction should I go in? If I follow it the wrong way, it will just lead me further and further into the forest.'

Pangur had no answer. Neither had Brendan. 'It's so quiet,' he said, more to hear the sound of his own voice than because he expected Pangur to respond.

'Better get those berries, eh?' he said, trying to make his voice sound braver. 'Of course, it might help if I knew what an oak tree looked like.'

There was no sun to guide him. The forest was very dark now, and had become an unholy tangle of thorny branches and swampy earth, sucking him down and pulling him back with every step he tried to take. The mist became thicker, shrouding the trees in ghostlike shapes. Pangur was also very nervous; she had jumped up on his shoulders and was peering around her fearfully. The only sound was the harsh voices of the black crows that swept in flocks over the forest, darkening the sky even more.

Now he was sure it was not his imagination. There were red eyes watching him from the branches. More than one. The more he looked the more eyes he could see. He struggled on, panicking, and heard himself sob with relief as he came to a clearing in the trees. There was a huge grey stone in the middle. He said to himself that if he climbed to the top of it he might be able to see over the mist and the trees, to where the Round Tower of Kells rose above its walls. And hopefully, he would be up so high that he would be safe from whatever creatures were watching him. But as he made his way across the grass of the clearing, the sky became darker still and the slitted red eyes moved out from their shelter in the trees. They surrounded Brendan and Pangur on all sides. He could smell them, a smell like the dogs of the monastery but much, much stronger. Pangur was hissing bravely, but she was as terrified as Brendan was himself. The creatures had started to snarl, dripping saliva from their great yellow teeth and red jaws, as if looking forward to a tasty meal. Brendan and Pangur were surrounded by a pack of black wolves.

4 aisling

The pack closed in tighter as Brendan tried to back away. But now he could go no further because his back was against the rock. Pangur leapt onto it and Brendan picked up a stick to defend himself, waving it madly, but it flew from his hand. His actions seemed to make the wolves angrier. Brendan clambered frantically onto the stone, scratching his arms and legs as he did so, and leaving a piece of his cloak caught in the snapping jaws of one of his pursuers. The red eyes of the wolves looked even more excited at the sight and smell of blood.

Suddenly, there was a high, piercing howl that seemed to shake the trees all around the clearing. The wolves stopped in their tracks, raising their heads. The sound seemed to be coming from behind the pack, and when Brendan looked over he saw the figure of what seemed to be another wolf outlined against the trees. It was much larger than any of the pack that had attacked Brendan. It also seemed to be white, snow white. The wolves began to shake. Then they began to whimper like puppies. Within seconds, every last one of them had taken to their heels, racing in all directions as if something had frightened the life out of them.

Brendan caught a glimpse of bright green eyes and sharp shining teeth. He lowered his head and put his hands together. There was nothing he could do now but pray.

Someone was speaking. 'Is this your cat?' It was a girl's voice, a young voice, and it sounded seriously annoyed.

Brendan opened his eyes and in front of him, instead of a slavering wolf, was a child. Pangur was in her arms and did not look too happy about it. Brendan stared at the girl, too surprised to answer her. Instead he tumbled down behind the stone, grabbed a twig he found there and waved it in the air, saying, 'I've heard about creatures like you. You're a fairy!'

The girl gave a snort and demanded, 'What are you doing in my forest? You've come to spoil it, haven't you?'

Brendan came out from behind the stone and stared at the girl. She was smaller and slighter than he was. Her hair was so long it swept to the ground. It was the colour of snow. The girl had bright green eyes, which were now slits of angry fire. She did not look at all pleased to see him.

Still stunned with shock, Brendan asked, 'What happened to the white wolf? Where did it go?'

'There's nobody here but me,' said the girl. 'And your cat.'

Pangur regarded the girl quietly, then went to Brendan and rubbed against him. The girl asked, 'What are you doing here? You were probably sent here by your family to get food, weren't you?'

Mist swirled around the clearing. The fairy-like figure jumped on top of the stone Brendan thought he had never seen any one able to jump like that – and continued, 'Well, you can go right back where you came from! If you don't, I'll make the wolves get you! You have no right to come here, disturbing the animals and the birds!'

'I didn't mean to,' said Brendan, his nerves in tatters from the way the girl kept jumping around the clearing, disappearing into the mist and then reappearing again.

'Look, I'm sorry, right? I'm not here to get food for my family. I'm here to get things to make ink. And I don't have a family and we have food in Kells! So I wouldn't come here for it anyway! I was just a bit lost and ...'

The girl, who had been walking away from him with her nose in the air, suddenly stopped.

'You don't have a family?' Her face seemed to soften a little. 'No mother?'

Brendan shook his head.

She said quietly, 'I'm alone too.' And then she disappeared into the trees.

Brendan ran after her, saying breathlessly, 'But my uncle looks after me. He's the Abbot of the monastery of Kells. And me and this other monk, his name is Aidan, we want to make a book, you see, and I need to get berries to make ink. Berries like this.' He opened his hand and showed the girl the berries Aidan had given him.

'What's ink?' asked the girl.

'It's hard to explain; it's like liquid colour and you put it on pages ... you would have to see it. But I have to get the berries.'

'Well you can't. You must leave.'

Brendan's mouth set into a stubborn line. 'I'm not leaving the forest until I get what I came for. I won't do any harm, I promise you. It won't hurt your old trees just to take a few berries. It's really important. The book we will make is so beautiful! We just need the berries to do it.'

The girl seemed to consider for a few moments, then said, 'Oh, all right then. I'll help you get the berries. If I don't help, you will probably spend ages rampaging through the forest and annoying the trees and unsettling everyone. But if I help you, you must promise me one thing.'

'What is it?' asked Brendan. He was a little bit afraid of this girl. He was sure she was one of the magical creatures he had been warned against. If she was magic, who knows what she might ask him. He had heard stories about the bargains magical beings made with humans. They never worked out well for the humans.

'I don't want you or your cat to come into my forest again. I don't want to see either of you here. You must promise me that you will not come back.'

Brendan didn't want to make the promise, and by the look on Pangur's face, she didn't want to either. But they really didn't have a choice, if they wanted to get the berries for Aidan. So, reluctantly, Brendan nodded. Then he said, 'My name is Brendan. What's yours?' But the girl just laughed and started to lead the way through the trees. Where there had just been grass before, there was now a carpet of snowdrops.

The sun had come out again, and they seemed to be following a path through the light. The girl was definitely magic, thought Brendan; otherwise how could she dart ahead so quickly? Sometimes she leapt halfway up the trunk of a tree as if she had wings; sometimes she glided along their upper branches like a squirrel. He would catch sight of her face looking down on him through a cradle of branches, laughing at his frightened expression.

'This is one of my favourite times in the forest,' she said. 'It's still very quiet, like it is in the winter, but everything is starting to grow and come to life again. I'll ask the forest where your berries are.'

As they made their way through the wood, she showed him many things that he had not noticed when he had been on his own. Walking with her was like having another pair of eyes, eyes that could see all the little things that it was so easy to miss: two beetles greeting each other on the stem of a fern, a nest of field mice snuggled in the bole of a beech tree, the hole in the earth where a badger lived. Finally, they came to a great tree, which seemed to stretch up high beyond all the others. Brendan could not even see the top.

'This is an oak. It's the oldest and tallest tree in the forest, and has special powers.'

She picked up a leaf that had fallen to the ground the autumn before.

'See, look, it has curly edges. And the berries you are looking for are growing on the tree.

Though they are not really berries, they are just things that grow on the oak.'

She stopped and looked at Brendan's face.

'The berries, as you call them, are up at the top,' she said. 'It's a big tree. You have climbed a tree before, haven't you?'

Brendan paused. This girl was smaller and younger than he was and the thought of climbing the tree didn't seem to bother her at all. How hard can it be? he thought.

So he said, 'Yes, of course. It's easy.'

He soon discovered it was not easy at all; in fact, climbing the huge oak tree was one of the most difficult things he had ever tried to do. Twigs and branches scraped his arms and legs and poked him in his eyes. His feet slid on the wet bark, unable to get a foothold. The one branch that he wanted to catch in order to go higher always seemed just a little beyond his reach. And the further up he climbed, the further there was to fall ...

The girl, on the other hand, scampered up the tree with the ease of a squirrel. Now she was really starting to irritate him. Why did she have to go so fast? He tried to climb more quickly, so that he could catch up with her, and found himself sliding and stepping onto thin air. He was falling down through the branches, and just when he thought his heart was going to stop, he managed to catch hold of a branch, which he clung onto for dear life. He looked up to where the girl was peering down at him through the leaves. She jumped easily onto the branch he was clinging to and pulled him up to safety.

'You're useless at this,' she said crossly. 'I thought you said you knew how to climb trees!'

'I do,' he said. 'Smaller ones.'

'Yeah,' said the girl. 'Like bushes?'

At last they reached the top of the tree. As the girl had said, the oak was the tallest tree in the forest. When he looked down, Brendan thought the ground was rushing up to meet him. His stomach turned over and he was sure he was going to be sick. Once again he could feel his legs going, his body lurching towards the ground below ... and the girl had to push him back against the trunk of the tree.

'Don't look down,' she told him, holding his

arm tightly. Brendan shut his eyes and tried to breathe.

After a moment, the girl said, 'Come on, Brendan, open your eyes now!'

He shook his head grimly and kept them shut.

'Come on,' she said again. 'Open your eyes and I'll tell you my name.'

Brendan opened his eyes.

'It's Aisling,' the girl said, 'and this is my forest.'

He looked down. He could see far into the distance in every direction. Away to the west, he could even see the encircling wall of Kells, with the great stone Round Tower rising in the centre. Inside the walls, he could make out the tiny figures of the monks, scuttling around as they worked. It reminded him of an anthill he had once disturbed. But the monastery was only a small break in the greenness that surrounded him on all sides.

'Have you ever been over there?' Brendan pointed over towards the monastery. 'That's Kells. That's where I live.'

Aisling shook her head. 'Never. I never leave my forest. I stay in the trees, and I never go inside walls. This is my place. And you had better be getting back to yours ... Look, the sun is already going down.'

She jumped down to a slightly lower branch and Brendan followed, much more slowly and cautiously. He suddenly noticed that there was a nest of wasps on the branch and pulled back, afraid he would be stung.

'They won't sting you!' said Aisling. 'I asked them not to!'

The wasps flew away and there, in a cluster, were the little brown berries that Aidan had shown him. It was hard to believe, thought Brendan, as he started to gather them and fill his satchel, that they could make the lovely green ink he had seen on the pages of the Book.

Aisling picked one and grimaced. 'They look like wild boar droppings!' she said.

'And they are really stinky!' added Brendan.

When he had finished gathering the berries, they scrambled down the tree, Brendan falling the last bit and feeling embarrassed by his clumsiness in front of the girl. But she just laughed.

To his surprise, Brendan discovered that he did not really mind her laughing at him any more.

'Now, I will lead you back,' Aisling said. 'We had better go the short way. But be sure to stick with me; there are dangerous things along the way ...'

She led the way along a different route back through the forest. This path was more difficult to follow. The trees grew more closely together and let in less light. Brendan and Pangur stayed close to the girl, who found her way as if it was the easiest thing in the world to make a track through the trees.

After a while, they came to a clearing. It was a strange place. Although there were no trees, there seemed to be even less light here than there had been among the thickets. On one side of the clearing, there was a wall of black rocks. Brendan stopped, fascinated by the sight of two great stone figures on either side of a dark opening in the rock. Pangur mewed loudly. Aisling, who had run ahead, looked back.

'Come away, Brendan,' she said, in a voice that suddenly sounded full of fear.

'Come away from this place. This is a place of suffering.'

'Suffering?' said Brendan 'What do you mean?'

'Just come away!' Aisling whispered. 'It's too dangerous!'

Brendan laughed. Now he felt that he was the brave one. 'Surely it can't be more dangerous than climbing an oak tree!'

Aisling grabbed him and tried to pull him back. 'It is the cave of the Dark One! Of Crom Cruach!'

'The Dark One?' said Brendan. 'Crom Cruach? But my uncle told me about the Crom worshippers. Crom Cruach is only pagan nonsense, a story, an imaginary thing. My uncle says that you shouldn't be afraid of imaginary things.'

Aisling gave a deep sigh. 'Brendan,' she said, 'you mustn't say its name too loud. It might hear you. It's waiting in the darkness, waiting for someone to wake it. Brendan, listen to me, you must come away now ...'

5 The Creature in the Darkness

But Brendan had moved closer to the entrance to the dark place. The two stone guardians stared at him out of blind eyes. They were roughly carved, but he could see that they were human figures. Their faces, crude as they were, still managed to look cruel. Brendan began to feel that their lips were moving, whispering something, calling him in.

Brendan could sense something pulling him towards the blackness. Nearer and nearer he went, fascinated by the draw of the dark.

Then he heard it. There was a sound, coming from the entrance. It was like something large and heavy shifting in the darkness. An animal, perhaps? If so, it would have to be a creature even bigger than the elephants Brother Assoua had told him about.

No, now there was a different sound, not like an animal. A slithering and a heavy sliding. As it grew louder, Brendan found something very strange was happening to him. His feet were bringing him closer to the cave while his mind screamed at him to get out of that place as fast as he could.

Aisling was crying now, still calling out to Brendan to come away. When he glanced at her – though he could hardly pull his eyes away from the entrance – her face had changed. It was no longer that of a little girl, but of an old, old woman, wrinkled with pain and fear. But even this sight could not make him turn from the cave's entrance. Nor could the fact that Pangur had her teeth dug into his sleeve and was frantically trying to pull him away, mewing pitifully.

The slithering noise continued. His heart thumping in his chest, Brendan realised that there was Something awake down there. He had woken the Thing that lived down in the darkness, and it was coming for him.

Now he was afraid, really afraid. He tried to

turn and run, but terror overcame him and he could not move. The sense of the blackness coming from the cave was growing stronger and stronger. And a wind was coming from the entrance, a wind that sucked him towards the cave, that was pulling him in despite himself.

Brendan realised that he was trapped, caught by the evil thing. He could do nothing but wait until he came face to face with the horror. And he knew, without a shadow of a doubt, that the one purpose that horror lived for was to destroy and to kill, to cause pain and sorrow and suffering.

Something bright came between him and the dark wind. Aisling had come to help him. With all her strength, she was pushing one of the stone statues across the entrance to the cave. How could she do it, she is so small? thought Brendan. How could she possibly shift one of those great stone creatures? But she did. With a cry like a scream, the stone fell to the earth, blocking the entrance so that whatever it was that lived down there could not come out.

The spell was broken. The wind stopped and

Brendan found he could move again. He rushed over to where Aisling lay panting on the ground. Pangur curled herself around the girl's neck, trying to warm her. Aisling's face was as white as her hair. Her eyes were closed and her lips looked blue, as if the blood had stopped in her body. Brendan wondered if the strain of pushing over the statue had killed her.

He said, frantically, 'Aisling, Aisling, wake up. Are you hurt?'

For a moment, nothing happened, but then Aisling shook her head. She slowly opened her eyes and Brendan asked, 'What was that?'

'I told you,' said Aisling, and her face was like an old woman's. 'Crom Cruach.'

They moved quickly from the clearing and as soon as they did, Aisling began to recover.

'That's the third time today I saved your life,' she said. 'I hope you are grateful. We had better go as fast as we can. If we don't hurry up, you will be in big trouble with that uncle of yours.'

As they walked through a forest lit by the red

glow of the evening sun, Brendan asked, 'What happened just now? Who is Crom Cruach?'

Aisling shuddered. 'I don't like to even mention his name. It poisons the air of the forest. But you had better know. You have to realise how dangerous he is. Just in case you think of doing something stupid like going back to that clearing.'

She paused and took a deep breath.

'Crom Cruach is one of the Old Dark Ones,' she said, whispering as if she did not want the forest to hear what she was saying. 'He has many different names, and many different lairs. Some people call him Crom Dubh, the Black One. Others say that his name means Bloody Head. There are those who think that it means Bloody Mound. He has existed since the beginning of time. Through the ages, he has ruled by fear, and he has taken many different shapes, many forms. One of the shapes he takes is that of a huge snake. A serpent, they say, with only one eye. There are some people who worship him out of fear. He has many ways in and out of the upper world. Sometimes he is not seen for years. But you heard something, didn't you?'

Brendan nodded. 'A kind of slithering noise ...'

Aisling closed her eyes for a moment. 'I think he is awake,' she said, her voice faint. 'Oh, I hope I'm wrong.'

'Oh, look,' she continued, sounding relieved to change the subject. 'We're nearly there. Can you see the walls of Kells? We will just about reach it before the sun goes down completely.'

They followed the wall to the secret entrance where Brendan had crept out that morning. It felt like a very long time ago to him – much longer than a day.

Now it was time to leave Aisling, Brendan discovered he didn't want to go. Pangur was already caught up in her arms, licking her goodbye.

Brendan said, 'I suppose you don't want to come in and see where I live?'

Aisling laughed. 'I do not want to go behind those walls,' she said. 'I told you, I belong to my forest. But you know what, I've changed my mind about something. You can visit the forest again, if you like ... and Pangur can come too.'

'But how will I find you?' asked Brendan.

'Don't worry, I'll find you,' said Aisling. 'Nothing happens in the forest without me knowing about it.'

They smiled at each other and Brendan and Pangur pushed their way through the gap into the enclosure.

Brendan couldn't wait to show Aidan the berries. He ran to the Scriptorium and burst through the door, waving the bag and almost babbling with excitement.

'Brother Aidan!' he began. 'I found them!' Then he stopped abruptly.

Uncle Cellach was in the Scriptorium. He seemed to be in the middle of an argument with Aidan. They both had their hands on one of the tables, as if to push it in a certain direction. All the other monks were standing around, looking upset. The Abbot was saying quietly, 'I don't care how you arranged the tables in Iona! Here it will be as I say!'

He turned to where Brendan stood in the doorway.

'Well, Brendan,' he said. 'It's about time we saw you today. Where have you been?'

Brendan said nothing, just hung his head. His uncle marched out of the Scriptorium and Brendan followed him, but before he left, he tried to signal to Aidan that he had managed to get the berries.

As they crossed the enclosure to the Round Tower, the Abbot said again, 'Well, I'm listening. Where were you?'

Brendan gulped. He knew he was going to get into huge trouble if he told the truth. But he couldn't lie to his uncle.

He said, quietly, hoping that his uncle might not hear, 'I … I went into the forest. Just for a little while. Just to get the berries for Brother Aidan, to make ink for the Book.'

His uncle stopped. He stood with his back to Brendan. His voice was calm.

'Brendan, have I not warned you enough about what lies outside these walls?'

Brendan tried to explain again that he had to go to the forest for the Book, but Cellach interrupted him.

'And yet you disobey me,' he said. He turned and faced Brendan, his voice still calm, but Brendan could see that he was very angry. 'You are never to leave the Abbey again without my permission. Do you understand?'

He stood staring at Brendan, who finally said, 'Yes.'

Abbot Cellach started to walk on again.

'Good,' he said. 'Now there are matters to be tended to in the workroom.'

But Brendan, as he followed his uncle and listened to what had to be done to improve the wall, kept the picture in his mind of how delighted Aidan would be when he showed him what he had brought him from the forest.

Aidan was more than delighted, he was ecstatic, when Brendan crept to the Scriptorium that night and presented him with the bag of berries. Then Brendan told him about his adventures, but although he mentioned to Aidan that a friend had helped him get the berries, he did not tell him Aisling's name or the fact that he was sure she was a magical being. For some reason he felt she would like him to keep her a secret, even from Aidan.

Aidan showed Brendan how to make ink from the berries. The first time he made the ink was quite an experience. Aidan ground down the berries to an evil-smelling paste. Then he boiled them up with other strange potions he took from his bag. He spent a long time pouring the mixture from one vial to another, talking and explaining as he worked.

'Now you and Pangur stay under the table for the moment, I'll tell you why later. Yes, this is going to be a good mix. Those were great berries you and your friend found for me. Now was it two vials of acid and one of mercury or the other way around? The old head is going ... that's for sure. Ah, nearly there ...'

He held up the cup and smiled. 'Finished!' he said.

BANG!

The liquid exploded, shaking the walls and roof of the Scriptorium. Green smoke filled the room.

Coughing, Brendan and Pangur crept cautiously out from under the table.

Aidan was standing there with the cup in his hand, his face black from the explosion and his eyebrows signed. His hair was singed too, but he was smiling widely. Brendan could only be grateful that his uncle was working on the other side of the monastery wall that day and so would not have heard the explosion.

'Ah, that's grand,' said Aidan uncertainly. 'Lots of smoke. That's a good sign.'

Aidan taught Brendan other things too, how to hold the pen steady and straight, how to touch the page as lightly as a bee's wing. He taught him how to draw the fabulous interlacings that decorated the Book. How every stroke was to be done for the love and glory of God and nature. He made Brendan realise that a line drawn well was as much an act of worship as building an abbey or saying a prayer. Sometimes Brendan made mistakes and felt tempted to give up, but Aidan always encouraged him to keep going.

While they worked, Aidan told Brendan stories of the saints. He told him about Patrick, the first of the great saints of Ireland, who had turned himself and his monks into deer in order to escape the attack of an angry king. He told him of Brigid, who used a sunbeam as a coathanger and whose symbol was the February snowdrop. He told him of Ailbhe, whose foster mother was a wolf, and who had invited her to dinner every day in his palace when he had become a great and powerful bishop. Brendan especially liked that one because of the wolf. He also loved Aidan's story about a French saint, called Austreberthe, who asked a wolf to carry the laundry for her convent, as he had eaten the donkey that used to do it for her. But Brendan's favourite story was the tale of Colmcille's horse.

When the saint was very old, his beautiful white horse, who had grown old with him, came to him one day and laid his head on his chest. And the horse had wept, because he knew that Colmcille was going to die soon. The other monks had wanted to send it away, but Colmcille had not let them, for he loved the animal very much. And also because it comforted him that the horse had realised something that even Colmcille's best friends in the monastery did not know.

But Aidan also told Brendan stories that were not about monks or saints. Stories about the magical beings who had lived in Ireland before the coming of Christianity. He told him how many of them had come and spoken to the saints about the glorious days gone by. About Oisín, child of the deer and son of Fionn, and the Swan Children of Lir, and about Lí Ban the mermaid, who had changed shape when the waters of Lough Neagh rose up and covered her kingdom. And because Aidan had studied Greek and Latin, some of the stories he told were wonderful tales about people who lived far away from Ireland.

Brendan once asked Aidan, 'But were they real people? Did those things really happen? My uncle says those are only imaginary things.'

And Aidan answered, 'Does he indeed?' Then he sighed. 'Your uncle is a very wise man, Brendan, but no more than anyone else in this world, he doesn't know everything. There are those that might say the faith that *we* believe in is no more than a story, and miracles a different sort of magic. But I have been here on this earth a long time now, Brendan, and there is something I am sure of. Just because you can see something doesn't mean it is real. And just because you cannot see something doesn't mean it isn't there. Enough of my blather. I don't want to be confusing you with all this talk. Let's get on with the work!'

During the day, Brendan went about his work, and helped with building the wall, which grew higher every day; but in the evenings, he would sneak out of his cell. He would go to the Scriptorium, where Aidan would be waiting to teach him. The other monks would help them, covering for Brendan when he was too sleepy to do the tasks the Abbot set him. They also found the raw materials for the inks and helped with making it. All of them wanted to see the Book completed.

Spring passed into summer and Brendan sometimes slipped out of the monastery with Pangur and met Aisling in the forest. In the woods, he learned as much as he did in the Scriptorium. Aisling taught Brendan all about the different trees of the forest, their natures, their strengths and their weaknesses and their special powers. She introduced him to the animals and birds, which would come to her without any fear. Most of all, she taught him how to see the beauty that was all around him.

The one dark cloud during that summer was that more and more refugees from the Northmen came to Kells, ragged and terrified, telling fearful tales of the cruelty and violence of the invaders. Each refugee had a story, and each story was sadder than the last. Parents came who had lost their children; children came who had lost their parents. Hundreds of innocent people had been killed or dragged away as slaves.

And at night, after he had seen another group of starving villagers seek refuge in the Abbey and listened to their stories, Brendan would sometimes wake up and find himself shaking with fear. He would have had the dream again, the dream of fire and smoke, of huge shadowy figures leaning over him, waving swords and axes. Of cruel laughter, of crackling flames and screams. Of trying to get away, but not being able to move. That nightmare had come to him from the time he was very small, and he sometimes wondered if it was partly a memory of what had happened to him when his people were attacked, when he was a tiny baby.

One night Aidan and Pangur came up to where Brendan was working and Aidan said to Pangur, 'Not bad. I'd say he could do it, right enough.'

Pangur miaowed in agreement.

Brendan looked up from where he was carefully sketching an angel's face. He had drawn the figure balanced on a green stem, sitting there in a way that reminded him of Aisling.

'Do what?' he asked, his mind still on his work.

Aidan went to the window and stood with his back to Brendan.

'I must confess, my boy, I haven't been completely honest with you. I cannot do the Chi Ro page. My eyes have become too old and my hands unsteady.'

He turned to Brendan. His face was very serious.

'You should be the one to do the Chi Ro page!'

6 the eye of colmcille

'**m**e?' Brendan could not believe his ears. 'I couldn't do the Chi Ro page! I'm only a boy! You are the master craftsman. You know what to do. If I tried to do it, I'd only ruin it ...'

'You know, I don't think you would,' said Aidan. 'I have watched you. It's not just that your eyes are as sharp and your hand is as steady as any I've ever seen. You have the gift of sight, my lad, of inner sight, of the eye of the imagination. Your only problem is that you are a bit afraid of it yourself. If you are ever to light up the Chi Ro page, you will have to face up to your fears. There is something stopping you from doing that, but if you do, you will be able to make something that will indeed be the work of angels.'

He paused.

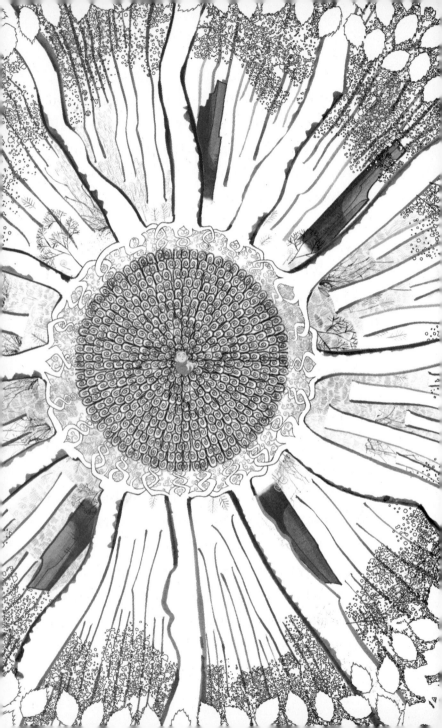

'Of course you will need something to help you. You will need another eye. Colmcille's Eye. Colmcille instructed that it should never be used unless the work was worthy of it. It has not been used since Iona. But I am sure that he would want it to go to you.'

'What?' said Brendan, 'The eye? Colmcille's eye? So it is true he had a third eye? I thought it was just a story, like the one about him having a third hand with twelve fingers!'

'I can assure you Colmcille had only two hands and the normal number of fingers. And the Eye isn't a real eye. At least it isn't a human eye. It is an eye of a very special kind,' said Aidan, starting to fumble in his satchel. 'It's called a crystal. It is the most beautiful and wonderful thing, wherever it's got to.' He paused and scrabbled a bit more in the satchel, looking more and more worried as he did so.

'But the power of the crystal is not just in its beauty. When you look through it, you can see details that even the sharpest-eyed person in the world could not see without it. It is amazing. You can see even down to the pattern on a bee's wing. That is how Colmcille managed to make such intricate designs. He kept the Eye hidden. Only a few monks, the ones closest to him, knew about it at all. That was partly to keep it safe, and partly because there are those who might have been afraid of it. They might have argued that it was not the Lord's will to see too closely. But Colmcille always said that there was nothing the Lord created that could not be used for the good or evil, and it was the choice of man to decide what way to use it. So the good or evil was in the man or woman using the thing, not the thing itself. And the Eye of Colmcille was always used to create beautiful things. When Colmcille lay dying, the Eye dropped from his hand. And since then it has been kept safe in the monastery. When Iona was attacked those were the two treasures entrusted to me by the other monks ... the Book and the Eye. But ...'

Suddenly, Aidan put his hands to his head in despair.

'I have lost it, and we cannot make the Book

without it! It's lost! It's all lost!'

Brendan had never seen Aidan like this and it
scared him.

'Where did you last have it?' he asked.

Aidan shook his head. He looked desperately
unhappy.

'I have no idea,' he said. 'I can't think what
might have happened. I so was sure it was safe in
the satchel. That's why I didn't even bother to look
for it before now. But now that I think of it, it must
have been when I fled from Iona. There was that
time when I was getting onto the boat, with the
Northmen right behind me. I have a vague
memory of dropping the satchel and something
falling then; it must have been the Eye. It could be
anywhere now, anywhere between here and Scotland. Crushed by the Northmen or lost at the
bottom of the sea ... I have failed, Brendan. Failed
in the task my brothers gave me.'

'Where did the Eye come from?' asked Brendan.
'Maybe we can get another one?'

Aidan shook his head.

'No, I'm afraid that is impossible. The story is

that the Eye was captured by Colmcille himself. He fought a great battle with a deadly serpent, one of the Old Ones, in order to win it. He nearly died in the battle, but in the end, he was victorious and sent the wicked snake howling and yowling deep into its lair under the waters of Lough Ness. Didn't I tell you our founder was a great warrior as well as a monk? While they fought, he pulled one of the monster's eyes from its head. He brought it to Iona.'

Aidan sat down heavily at the Scriptorium table and buried his head in his hands.

Pangur came up to him and rubbed her body against his arms, trying to comfort him. Aidan continued:

'Some say that before the crystal became known as the Eye of Colmcille, it had an ancient name. Named for the creature that Colmcille won it from. It was called the Eye of Crom Cruach.'

Brendan gasped, remembering Crom Cruach's cave and the way he had been pulled towards its terrible darkness.

Aidan sat for a moment with his head in his

hands. Then he looked up and rubbed his eyes wearily. He began to draw the crystal on a piece of parchment.

'I can't tell you which parts of the story are true. But the Eye looked like this.'

He showed the picture to Brendan. It was a strange, many faceted pattern which somehow terrified Brendan. And yet it reminded him of the designs that had been carved on the entrance to the cave of the Dark One. He placed his hand on it to hide it; but when he lifted his hand, the Eye stared back at him, imprinted on his palm. He shivered. Aidan was looking into the fire, his shoulders bent in sorrow. His voice was shaking when he spoke.

'I have failed you too, Brendan, for you could have used the Eye to create something that would be treasured forever. I am just a useless old man ...'

'You are not,' said Brendan. He tried to think of something else he could say to make Aidan feel better. But there was nothing to say.

That night, as darkness lay over the monastery,

Brendan slipped from his bed and pulled on his cloak. Pangur sat in front of him, meowing in a worried way.

'I know it will be dangerous,' Brendan said to her. 'But it was Crom Cruach that Colmcille fought, and that is why Crom Cruach has only one eye. So his other eye must be a crystal too. And it's up to me to get it so that the Book can be finished ...'

He shivered. Even the thought of going back to that dreadful place in the woods where Crom Cruach had his den was enough to make the hairs on the back of his neck rise up in fear. But I have to get it, he thought; Aidan is too old and there is nobody else to do it.

Even if I do manage to do it, he thought ruefully, and am not killed by the monster, Uncle will probably kill me anyway if he finds out I've left the monastery again. But somehow the thought of his uncle's anger no longer seemed so frightening. He moved carefully to the door of his room. Picking Pangur up and cuddling her, he said, 'Don't worry, Pangur, I won't be alone. But it is too dangerous to bring you along this time. You stay here and mind Aidan while I'm gone.'

Brendan left the tower and began to creep down the steps into the mist, looking back to make sure that Pangur had stayed behind. And so, not looking where he was going, he walked straight into a tall figure. There, blocking his way and looking angrier than he had ever seen him, was the Abbot. His uncle's voice was very cold when he said, 'And where do you think you are going?'

Brendan gulped and said nothing.

'This has gone on long enough, Brendan. It has to stop. You will have to learn obedience. That is one of the great lessons of this life. Not to question those who know better. You have been getting worse, more foolhardy and disobedient by the day. Especially since you started spending time with Brother Aidan, who no doubt has been putting all sorts of ideas into your head. You have been forbidden to leave the Abbey. Now you are forbidden to enter the Scriptorium. You are forbidden to speak to Aidan, and you are forbidden to paint or draw or illustrate. Your days will be spent doing chores or helping with the wall. Is that clear?'

'Crystal,' muttered Brendan, thinking of the Eye. But he couldn't leave it at that. He had to try to make his uncle understand. He began, 'But Uncle, just let me explain ...'

Cellach interrupted him. 'There is no need for explanations. I understand perfectly well. I understand that you are a wilful, disobedient little boy with a head full of dreams and nonsense! I understand that every day the Northmen come closer to us and that the work on the wall cannot be delayed by dreamers and artists! Now it is *you* who must understand. No more excursions, no more Scriptorium, and no more Brother Aidan!'

The Abbot started to walk away from Brendan.

Brendan looked at his back and said quietly, 'No.'

The Abbot turned around and Brendan looked stubbornly at the ground. It had cost him all of his courage to say that one small word to his uncle.

'What did you say?' The Abbot's voice was as cold as winter.

'I can't do that. I can't give up the Book.' Brendan could feel tears coming to his eyes but he kept talking. 'If you would only look at it, at one page of it, you would know why I have to keep making it. It's so beautiful.'

He paused. For a moment, he thought his uncle was going to relent. He continued eagerly, 'You must realise how important it is; it's much more important than the wall. You used to make art yourself ... Brother Aidan said you were an illuminator once ...'

But Brendan had gone too far and the Abbot lost patience. 'That's enough!' he said sharply. He grabbed Brendan by the arm and pulled him down the stairs to the little cell in the bottom of the tower, where he banged the door behind him and locked him in. 'If I can't trust you to stay out of harm's way, you will have to remain here until you see sense.'

He sighed, and said more quietly, 'I don't want to do this, believe me. But it's a hard and dangerous world, Brendan. Making pretty drawings is not going to save you from all the bad things that can happen. I wish you could realise that. I'm going to Brother Aidan now, to get that accursed book from him and lock it away somewhere. Somewhere where it won't take everyone's mind off the work they are supposed to be doing. Every monk in the place is distracted and Aidan is the cause of it all. That man has caused nothing but trouble since he came here ... And as for you, you can stay there until you learn a bit of respect and obedience. Until then, I wash my hands of you.'

He began to make his way upstairs. Brendan was left listening to the angry swish of his cloak on the stone as he walked quickly up the steps.

7 The Rescue

Brendan looked around him. The cell was damp and bare. There was very little furniture: just a wooden table, a three-legged stool, and a straw pallet to sleep on. There wasn't even a fireplace. Brendan's only company appeared to be a nest of baby mice and a very busy spider, intent on creating a web between the rafters. Brendan examined every corner, but he could not find any way out of the cell. Faint light came in from a tiny barred window high up on one wall. He pulled over the stool and climbed onto it, peering out. The window looked out at ground level so all he could see were the monks' feet passing by. They had started the day's work on the wall. Brendan recognised Brother Jacques's bony toes and called out to him, but he did not stop. All the monks knew that the Abbot was in a terrible mood today and were going about their tasks as quickly as possible.

Watching the passing feet, the mouse family and the spider and wondering how he could get out was Brendan's only entertainment all day. In the evening, Brother Tang came to the door with a meal of soup and oatcakes and buttermilk for him. Tang was sympathetic, but said to Brendan, 'It's more than my life is worth to let you out, my child. The Abbot is like a demon today. He is pushing himself – and all of us – to work on the wall as if there were no tomorrow. I'm telling you, he will end up killing himself if he keeps going like this. And he has had a dreadful row with Brother Aidan. We have never seen anything like it in Kells. He tried to take the Book from him! But Brother Aidan just spoke very quietly and said to Abbot Cellach that the Book had been put in his keeping. That minding it was a sacred task given to him by the dead brothers of Iona. So in the end Abbot Cellach left it with him. But he told Aidan he would have to leave Kells when the first thaw of spring comes.'

'Leave Kells?' said Brendan. 'But where will he go to be safe? And he can't leave here. We have to finish the Book.'

Tang sighed. 'Yes, what are we going to do about the Book? All of the brothers want to see it finished. That is why many of us came to Kells, you know. Because it was known as a place of great learning and a centre of illumination. We had heard of the marvellous work that was being done and we wanted to be part of it. And now we have ended up as stonemasons and builders. But there, I have said too much. It is not for me to question the Abbot's will. Eat up your dinner now. I'll be with you in the morning with some breakfast. And Brendan, try not to look so sad.'

He turned to go, and then turned back to Brendan and asked him, 'By the way, is Brother Aidan's cat with you? She's been missing all day and he's very worried about her.'

'No, I haven't seen her since I was locked up,' said Brendan, wondering what Pangur was up to.

Brendan couldn't eat his dinner, even though he realised that Brother Leonardo had tried to make it especially nice for him. The food stuck in his throat so he fed the oatcakes to the mice.

I have to do something, he thought. I have to go to the forest and get Crom Cruach's Eye so the Chi Ro page can be written ... But here I am stuck inside these walls with no way out.

He felt angry tears come to his eyes. Why couldn't he make the Abbot see how important it was to finish the Book? How important it was to give people hope? To let them know that the times of beauty and peace would return? To reassure them that there was more to life than terror and darkness?

He lay huddled in the dusk, listening to the voices of the monks singing in the church, and later still to the sound of a blackbird singing from the forest. And when darkness fell and the moon rose, shedding its pale light through his little barred window, he heard a strange noise. He started up and went to the window, where he climbed up to the bars to peer out. What could it be? Listening carefully, he could make out that the voice was calling his name, and something white had appeared at the grating. In fact, two white things appeared: one was Pangur Bán, looking very proud of herself, and the other was Aisling, looking pale. She was not at all happy to be inside the walls of the monastery.

'Hello, Brendan,' she said. 'Happy to see us?'

'You could say that!' said Brendan, grinning from ear to ear with delight. 'But how did you find me? How did you know I was here?'

'Pangur was very brave,' said Aisling, stroking the cat, who purred loudly. 'She came to find me in the forest, to let me know you were in trouble and needed help. Now, how can I get you out?'

Brendan sighed heavily. 'The door of the cell is locked and bolted from the outside, and the Abbot has the key of the tower. He keeps it in his bedroom, hanging up on the wall. And he sleeps at the top of the tower. He has shutters on the window so the moon won't keep him awake. And he is a very light sleeper. He wakes up at even the slightest noise; you would have to be as quiet as a mouse or as quiet as Pangur here, to get the key. Maybe you should get Aidan? Maybe he could help?'

Aisling shivered and then said something very

strange, 'I'm sorry, Brendan. I couldn't do that. For a start, most likely Aidan would not even be able to see me. But I have another idea. Stay where you are. I won't be long.'

'Don't worry, I won't be going anywhere,' said Brendan gloomily. He peered after Aisling and saw her leap lightly away. Then she came back and picked Pangur up. Just before she disappeared, with Pangur clasped in her arms, she turned to Brendan and said, 'The Abbot has shut out the moon, but he can't shut out the mist.'

Brendan sat by his window in the moonlight, waiting for Aisling and Pangur to return. Despite himself, his eyes began to close, and from far away it seemed to him as if he could hear the sound of singing. The singing crept into his mind, winding through it like a trail of ivy, opening pictures in his head. He could see Aisling and Pangur as they made their way to where the Abbot slept in his tower, Aisling gliding up the stone wall with Pangur clasped around her neck. There, through the gap in the shutters, he could see his uncle lying

fast asleep. He was snoring a little and he had a frown on his face. On the wall beside him hung a large key. Aisling began to sing softly to the cat.

You must go where I cannot
Pangur Bán, Pangur Bán
Níl sa saol seo ach ceo
is ní bheimíd beo
ach seal beag gearr.

As she sang, a mist grew and swirled around Pangur. The cat seemed to lose her solid, furry form and became a creature of mist and shadows.

And the mist cat made her way through the gap in the shutters. As the cat took the key from its place on the wall, the Abbot moaned gently in his sleep. Brendan stirred in his dream state, afraid that his uncle would wake up. But the Abbot only muttered something about a wall and Pangur came back to Aisling, the key held safe in her mouth.

The music continued, but then another noise jerked Brendan out of his dream. It was the noise of a latch being lifted. And there was the mist Pangur, with the key of the tower in her mouth. Brendan let himself out quickly and made his way past the sleeping monastery. The mist-cat slid away back to the tower where she replaced the key beside the sleeping abbot.

When Brendan reached the secret entrance in the wall, he found that Aisling was waiting for him on the other side.

Brendan was so delighted to be out of the tower that he gave Aisling a hug.

'Hug Pangur if you like,' said Aisling. 'She's the one who did the work. But listen, why did the Abbot lock you up?'

'Because I disobeyed him. He caught me trying to go to the forest.'

'Why? To come to see me?'

'Not just that,' said Brendan. 'I wanted to go into the forest to find this.'

He raised his hand, and Aisling leapt backwards in fear.

'The Eye of Crom!'

'That's what it looks like, doesn't it?' said

Brendan. 'But it is actually a crystal. There was once another crystal just like it. Colmcille used it to make the most beautiful drawings in the world. It was lost on Aidan's journey to Kells, and he says we need another one. We can't finish the Book without it. I think there is one in the Dark One's cave. I have to go there.'

Aisling sat down suddenly on the ground, as if her legs had given way from under her.

'Fight Crom Cruach! You cannot do that! You cannot go there! The monster kills everything it touches!'

'I have to, Aisling', said Brendan. 'I have to try, at least.'

'No, Brendan, you don't understand,' said Aisling. 'Crom Cruach took my people. It took my mother. It is all-powerful. Even your saints, Colmcille and Patrick, could not kill it; they could only send it deeper into hiding. It is the thing that crouches and waits in the darkness, which lies there forever, waiting to strike. It is Crom Cruach, Crom Dubh, the Black Crooked thing. You are only a little boy. You couldn't even climb a tree before I showed you how. You have not much strength and you have no magic. Please, don't even try to do this.'

Brendan's looked into Aisling's pleading face. He felt a pain in this chest as he thought of his own mother. He was sorry to upset Aisling, but he knew what he had to do.

'If we do not get the crystal, the Book will never be finished. Aidan told me that the crystal lets you see things you would never be able to see with just your own eyes. Imagine, being able to see the pattern on a greenfly's wing or the veins on a blade of grass. I want to bring all those things to the Book, so that others can see it; and this is the only way to do it. You don't have to come with me. Maybe it is better if you don't. I don't want you to get hurt. But if you don't, I will still have to try to do it alone. I have to do it for the Book.'

They sat in silence for a moment. Aisling was crying, and Pangur was trying to lick the tears from her face, winding around her, comforting her with loud purring.

At last, Aisling pushed her long hair back from

her face and said, 'Alright then. I will help you. I will do it for you, and I will do it for the Book. And I will do it for my forest, because it will never be free of fear as long as Crom Cruach lies waiting underground at the heart of the wood.'

But her face had a frightened look that made her seem not like a little girl but someone much, much older.

8 crom cruach

The forest seemed a very different place in the nighttime. The darkness drained it of colour. The shapes of the trees stood out sharply, like black charcoal lines against the brighter sky. A fox cried, its head up, and crows swooped through the gloom, their outline clear against the full moon. Aisling led the way and they moved deeper and deeper into the shadows, away from the moon's brightness. As they went further into the wood, it grew colder, unnaturally cold. Pangur kept close by them, paying no attention to the rustling noises of small animals, the mice and hedgehogs going about their nightly business in the undergrowth.

Finally, they reached the clearing with the cave mouth and the stone figures. Brendan shivered when he saw the entrance stones, carved with the eye pattern that he now had on his palm. One of the stone figures was still upright; the other lay on the ground where Aisling had pushed it down. It still blocked the entrance to the cave, and through the summer, vegetation had grown over it. Not ordinary vegetation, not the nettles and briars and long grass that grew everywhere else in the forest, but something dark and slimy and foul-smelling, as if the darkness from under the earth was trying to creep out. Here even the moonlight had a greenish tinge; not the bright fresh green of the forest but a murky green, as if something had begun to rot. There was a smell too, a smell that reminded Brendan of hot days in Leonardo's kitchen when meat had begun to go off. But it was not hot; it was horribly cold and still.

'No life,' whispered Aisling. 'No life.'

Pangur leapt into her arms and snuggled down there as if she wanted to be somewhere else entirely.

For a moment, fear gripped Brendan. Was this really the only way to find a crystal like Colmcille's? Wasn't he crazy to try to fight a monster that great and saintly warriors had not managed to destroy? As Aisling had said, he was only a little boy. Surely there was no point in trying to do something that was this hopeless? Then he remembered something. The Abbot had once told him the story of how his parents and all his people had fought the Northmen. It was hopeless, but they had continued to fight. And maybe that was how the invaders had missed finding him. Maybe that was how he had survived. Now it was his turn to do something that seemed hopeless. There was no other way to go but forward – into the darkness of the cave.

He looked back at Aisling. She had set Pangur down. Her face was grey; her eyes huge; her body slumped like an old woman's. She was shivering uncontrollably.

Brendan ran back to her and wrapped his cloak around her shoulders.

'Aisling, you must go back,' he said. 'This place is hurting you. I'll go on alone. Bring Pangur with you, she's terrified.'

But Aisling shook her head. 'I must help you,' she said.

She went over to where the stone blocked the entrance and began to push. Brendan ran to help her. But before he could reach her, she had used every last inch of her strength to raise the figure upright so that the entrance to the cave was open again. And just as she finished, the wind started.

It was the wind that had tried to suck Brendan in once before. He was being pulled forward. He could see that beside him Aisling was also being pulled into the darkness, although she was resisting with all her strength. His cloak was blowing about her shoulders, and her hair was the one spot of brightness in the blackness all around.

He tried to run towards her to help her, but then she faded into wisps of mist and moonlight, and now he himself was being pulled into the cave's mouth ... It seemed to Brendan that he was being buffeted and blown like a feather in the centre of a dark whirlwind. He was being pulled further and further in, falling down into blackness.

Then the wind stopped. Brendan was standing on dark stone deep inside the cave. He held up his torch. The walls around him were lit by a faint green glow. The dreadful smell that had filled the clearing was much stronger here. It smelled as if dead bodies had lain here for a long, long time.

Brendan tried to keep from swallowing the foul air into his lungs and looked around him. There were strange designs painted and carved on the walls of the cave. The patterns were not unlike the spirals and circles, the lozenges and triskels and interlacings that were part of the patterns Brendan had seen, and indeed helped to draw, in the Book. But here the message they carried was not one of goodness and hope. Here they meant something evil. He could feel it coming out of the walls. There were bones scattered around the cave too. He did not look too closely at them as he had a horrible feeling that some of them might belong to humans.

There was one pattern, one image that was bigger and more vivid than any of the others. It lay at the centre of the maze of patterned walls. It was a bright livid green, the green of frogspawn and lichen. No, not frogspawn. More like the skin of some huge serpent, coiled around the walls of the cave. Each scale was so delicately etched that it seemed almost lifelike.

Brendan felt his head begin to spin. Was it Crom Cruach's body, curled around the inside of the cave? If only, he thought, I had at least brought a weapon with me, a knife from the kitchen or a stick from the forest.

At his feet a crack opened and Brendan was falling again, through swirls and spirals of pattern. It felt to him as if he had moved into some other dimension, where he was falling through water rather than air.

Yet it was not real water, because he could breathe in it with difficulty. He tried to swim upwards through the blackness. He looked at the shape on his hand; it was glowing, like a torch in the darkness, and now it showed the serpent Crom. His eye followed the length of the coiled serpent to the small, evil head. Its eyelid was closed as if it was sleeping. The head moved up slowly, sniffing the wind; the red, forked tongue flickered out of the great mouth. The head turned slightly. Was raised up. The creature had scented him. Scented his fear. Its eye opened, a glistening crystal, a shining focus of white fire. The creature twisted and coiled around the walls, encircling Brendan on all sides. He lashed out with his hands.

As Brendan looked into the eye it seemed to mesmerise him, draw him into its depths. He forced himself to turn his head away from it. But as he did, his heart nearly stopped. He felt something at his legs, and he realised that the green and silver coils were moving, wrapping themselves around his feet and flicking him into the air, like a cat playing with a mouse.

Brendan's blood was beating in his head, like some kind of wild and frightening music, as he was buffeted and thrown through the darkness. A piece of chalk fell out of his pocket, and he grasped it in his hand.

From somewhere Aidan's voice came, as if Brendan were back in the Scriptorium and his friend was urging him to let his mind go free:

'Use your imagination, lad, your imagination can do anything, can go anywhere. Let it free.

There's something holding you back from letting it go. Unless you turn around and look at what that is, you will never be free of it ...'

And suddenly Brendan was in the forest, surrounded by the green leaves of summer, and he could hear Aisling whispering to him:

'Look at the leaves, Brendan, look at how the green shoots fight their way through the rock. The leaves are so weak, Brendan and the rock is so hard. But the flowers and the leaves come back every year, even through the stone. They are the strong ones ... they come back. You can be as strong as a leaf, as brave as a blade of grass. You must turn the darkness into light!'

And then, most surprisingly of all, he was in the Cellach's study and he could hear the Abbot's voice:

'You know there will come a day when it will be up to you, Brendan, to do what has to be done. There will be no one else to do it.'

He took hold of those three things: the power of the imagination and the hope of the forest and the strength that comes to those who take up the hopeless task because there is no one else to do it. And he found that he was not unarmed after all. He began to do the only thing he could think of doing; he began to draw.

Frantically, as Crom Cruach writhed and coiled, Brendan took the chalk and drew lines and circles around the serpent, caging it in. With each line he drew, the monster became more and more enraged. Brendan turned and twisted, wriggling as the serpent tried to wrap its coils tighter around his body. He realised that he could look the monster in the eye, the shining crystal that shone out in the midst of all the darkness of the cave.

As Brendan twisted and turned the chalk flew out of his hand and fell down into the black space. It was then Brendan discovered he had been pulled so close to the shining eye that he could reach up and grab it. He took the monster's eye with both his hands, forcing his fingers into the slime under the lids. The evil head started to fling itself backwards and forwards, trying to escape Brendan's grip. It was doing its best to strike him with its poisoned tongue. Brendan held on. He

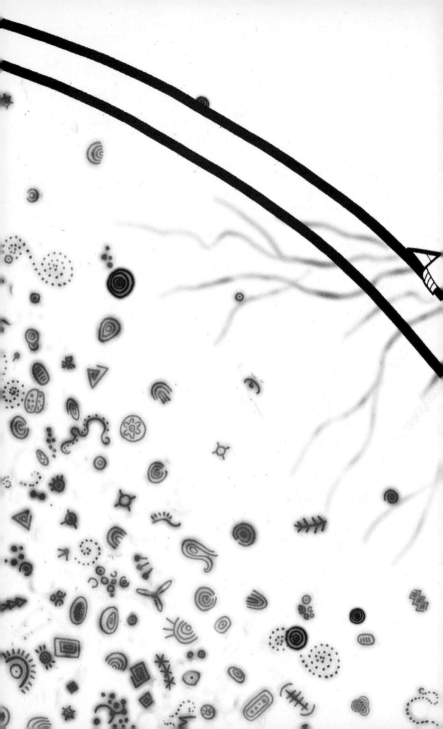

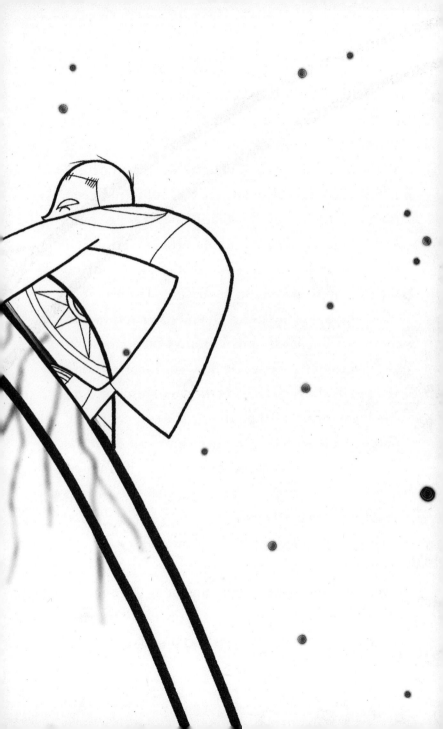

held on and pulled as hard as he could.

The monster flung him backwards and forwards with all the power of its body. It was hissing so that great clouds of foul black steam came from its mouth. Brendan knew that he could not keep his grip any longer. But that he had to. He could feel the eye burning his hands as he pulled, as if it were made of fire. In spite of the pain and the terror that gripped him, he did not let go.

As the eye came loose, the monster writhed in agony, coiling itself tighter around Brendan, seeking to crush his bones. It howled a fearful noise that made the rock walls of the cave shudder. And finally, with a roar of pain from the serpent and of shock from Brendan, the eye came out from the socket. Red gore dripped and hissed as it dropped into Brendan's arms, but the eye itself was as hard and bright as a diamond.

Brendan had done it. He had pulled the eye from the monster's head.

He fell back, watching in horror as the monster twisted madly. Blind now, it groped in the darkness with its head, trying to find Brendan so that it could catch him in its mouth. But as Brendan watched, the serpent, maddened with pain and rage, caught up its own tail and began to swallow itself, mistaking its own flesh for that of Brendan's. And so it swallowed frantically and continued to swallow and swallow, until it finally stopped. There was nothing left of Crom Cruach except a green circle of scales and mouth. The monster had destroyed itself. Brendan blacked out.

When he came to, he was at the mouth of the cave. Brendan wondered if he had simply dreamed the terrible battle. And yet the crystal was in his hand, caught in the blaze of dawn sunlight that lit up the clearing and made it a place of beauty rather than horror. The black leaves had gone from the trees. The grass of the clearing was covered in small white flowers.

'Aisling!' Brendan called anxiously, looking around him in an attempt to find her. There was no sign of the little girl. But there was a sign from her. Where Aisling had fallen there was a carpet of white snowdrops on the green grass, and lying on it was his cloak. On the cloak, there was a single white flower.

Pangur and Brendan looked at each other. Silently, the boy and the small white cat started to make their way back to the monastery. The sun was rising, lighting up the sky into red and gold and pink, and all the colours of the late summer forest seemed to be celebrating the defeat of Crom Cruach, the dark one who had kept the forest in a cage of fear for so many long years.

9 The eye of crom

On his journey back to the monastery, it seemed to Brendan that he could still hear Aisling's voice in his head. She was telling him the way back home. He could hear other voices too, and his eyes seemed to see things he had not seen before. He had somehow come closer to being part of the forest. He could feel the life it had lived for the thousands of years during which its trees had grown and died into the earth and grown again. Faces peered through the branches, but they did not frighten him, as they might once have done. They reminded him of Aisling. She was all around him. He saw a white raven with green eyes. It was Aisling. In a pool in the stream, a silver salmon swam and caught the nuts that fell from the branch above. By the flash of its silver scales, he knew it too was Aisling. A young deer, pale as snow, disappeared between the dark trees – Aisling again.

'She is still here,' he whispered to Pangur. 'She is still part of the forest. And the forest is safe now.'

Finally, they reached the grey stone walls of the monastery. Everything was very still and quiet. In an hour or so, all the brothers would rise to sing in the new day, but for the moment, they all slept.

However, not everyone was asleep. A light burned in the Scriptorium. Brendan made his way carefully up the stairs and peeped in through the door. Aidan was seated alone at the table where they had worked together. He was surrounded by inkhorns and brushes, but he was not doing anything. His head was in his hands and the Book was in front of him. It was open at a blank page. The page that he had told Brendan was to become the Chi Ro page. He was muttering quietly to himself.

'Oh, I'm only an old fool. I've made a right mess of things with my interference. I'll never be able for the work. I'll make a pig's ear of it for sure.'

He raised his head but did not see Brendan.

Pangur had come over to him, and he began to stroke her ears gently.

'So you are back, are you, you wild yoke. Out on the tear all night. And now you're soaked. What were you up to? I was worried about you. It's a pity you can't draw, Pangur, you would probably do a better job than me ... Brendan could have done it. Brendan could have made a masterpiece. But Brendan won't be let out by Cellach unless he promises to stop drawing ... oh, I should never have interfered. Old fools should learn to keep quiet ...'

'Unless young fools want to listen,' said Brendan quietly. Aidan looked up, his face full of joy.

'Boy!' he said. 'How did you get here? How did you get out of the tower?'

His face suddenly dropped, as if he was remembering his encounter with the Abbot.

'This is not the place for you, lad. You must go back to the tower before the Abbot finds out. There is nothing for you here.'

Brendan moved towards him.

'But you are here,' he said. 'The Book is here,' he

continued. 'And,' he paused, holding out his bundle, 'the Eye is here!'

Aidan took the bundle from Brendan and opened it slowly. Then his eyes widened in astonishment.

'How is this possible? The Eye was destroyed.'

'It's a long story,' said Brendan as he held the Eye up into the light, and the facets caught the glow and shone so brightly that they both blinked. But even when it was taken away from the light, the crystal still seemed to glow with a white, inner fire.

'The Dark One had more than one eye, you know!' Brendan explained. 'And more than one home!'

'What? What do you mean? You entered the Dark One's cave? You took the Eye from Crom Cruach's head? How did you ...?'

Brendan laughed. 'You can't find everything in books, you know!'

Aidan smiled back. 'I think I read that some-where once,' he said.

Then Brendan told Aidan the story of his

adventures in the cave of the Dark One. He also told him about Aisling's part in the story and her disappearance.

'Who is she, Aidan?' he asked. 'She seems to be able to take all sorts of shapes. And she hated having to come inside the walls of the monastery. Why was that? I know she is not evil, but she is not one of us, either.'

'You are right. She is not like us. But she is not human. She's one of the Old Ones too, like Crom Cruach. But she is one of the bright ones, Brendan, the ones that walk in the light and do good rather than evil. I do not know very much about the Old Ones, but I do know that they do not go away entirely; they only change their form. So she will come back, and she left the flowers as a sign for you. I am sure you will see her again some day. Maybe when you are least expecting it, maybe in some shape – an animal or a bird – that you will not recognise at first. But never let anyone make you think she is anything other than good.

She is part of the goodness of the trees and the wind, and of the creatures of the wood. Colmcille knew that, when he talked to the wild things. And the other saints too. Do you know that Kevin had a wolf as a friend? And when a bird laid an egg in his hand he didn't move until the little thing was hatched out and able to fly away on its own. And St Ciaran saved a fox from hunters, and in gratitude, the fox used to carry his prayer book for him when he went to mass. And St Mochua, now, he had mouse to wake him for his prayers, and a fly to walk along under the line of his prayer book and help him in his reading ... But here I am blathering on, and you must be exhausted by your great adventures. You are after turning out to be as great a hero, as great a warrior, as Colmcille himself!'

'Ah, I'm no hero. And honestly, I'm not a bit tired,' said Brendan. 'I wouldn't be able to sleep if I went to bed.'

'In that case, lad, do you feel up to getting to work?'

Brendan nodded eagerly.

Aidan picked up the crystal. 'Aye,' he said, 'it has the same power. But as I thought,' he squinted through it, 'it may be even better and clearer than the Eye of Colmcille. This one will be the Eye of Brendan. Look through it now, and tell me what you see.'

Brendan took the Eye and looked at one of the pages in the Book. With it, he could see details he had not been able to see before. It seemed to bring the tiny pictures alive.

'It's wonderful! If I use it for the smallest of small details I will be able to make the pictures even more beautiful,' he exclaimed.

Aidan nodded. 'That's right. Are you ready?' he asked.

'I think so. I hope so,' said Brendan.

'Then let us begin,' said Aidan.

He took up a quill and held it out to Brendan, who took it from him. Quietly and confidently, he began to draw.

Through the rest of the autumn, Brendan worked on the Chi Ro page. Using the crystal, he could see things that were invisible to the human eye. Sometimes he felt he really had a third eye, for with the crystal he could see the detail of an insect's wing or a spider's web, of a blade of grass, of a brown oak leaf, or the heart of a flower. It was slow, painstaking work, and although Brendan spent hours in the Scriptorium, even after weeks of work he had only a small corner of the page finished.

All this time his uncle thought that he was still locked in the cell at the bottom of the tower. Abbot Cellach asked Brother Tang to make sure the boy was warm and well fed. He was allowed out of the cell a few times a day to help in the gardens. Tang, or one of the other monks, was to keep a careful eye on him at all times. The Abbot gave strict instructions that he did not wish to see Brendan unless he was ready to promise not to see Aidan or go to the Scriptorium, and each time he asked Tang if this was the case Tang shook his head. The rest of the monks knew that Brendan spent most of his time with Aidan. They helped to smuggle him in and out of the cell. The monks brought him berries for ink and feathers for quills. They came and looked at the Book and stood in awe of Brendan's skill.

'It's like Heaven,' they said. 'It is the work of angels!'

'You are a better illustrator, a hundred times better illustrator, than any of us,' said Leonardo. Brendan didn't know what to say.

'It's not me, it's the Eye,' he said finally.

'No, child,' said Aidan. 'It is not just the Eye. It is your own inner eye that has the imagination to see these wonders.'

The winter came. It was a cold winter, so cold, with the frost so hard, that everyone said that the Northmen would surely not come to Ireland until the spring thaws. There were rumours that they had gone back to their own cold countries. Ships had been seen, sailing away over the wild ocean, laden down with gold and silver and precious stones and even more precious children from the Irish monasteries and villages that they had plundered.

The wolves howled in the forest, and the birds no longer sang, except for the black crows which cawed warnings of disaster from the trees and the single robin that would come to the Scriptorium window and watch Brendan at work on the Chi Ro page. In turn, Pangur would watch the robin as it sat there, planning to pounce, but the robin was always too quick for her. Pangur had slightly better luck with the mice that sometimes ran across the floor. Brendan and Aidan had to rescue quite a few of the small, soft creatures from her sharp teeth and claws.

Brendan was happy, although he missed Aisling. He still slipped into the forest when he could, but he never managed to see her. So instead, he watched the changes in the forest through the seasons. The trees that changed from glorious reds and yellows and coppers to the stark beauty of bare branches, to the absolute stillness of winter, gave him new ideas every day for his work.

And as Brendan worked on the Book, his uncle worked on the wall, and it grew higher and higher, until it blocked out the sun and the whole monastery lived in its shadow. There was only one entrance, a great wooden gate that was kept heavily barred and bolted. It was rarely opened. But as winter came in, more refugees from the raids of the Northmen arrived. It began to seem as if the icy cold and rough seas had not stopped their terrifying raids. The lines on the Abbot's face deepened and increased and he worked as hard as any of the monks on the wall. Indeed, he worked harder, as if he was punishing himself for something. During the evening, he sometimes went to the door of the tower, where he thought Brendan was still locked away, and listened. The monks watching him thought that he might open it, and held their breath in fear. But he never did. At the last moment he would turn away and go back to work on the wall.

'A stubborn child, that Brendan,' he would say to Tang. Tang would reply quietly, 'I wonder who he got that from, Brother Abbot?'

10 The darkness from the sea

It was a snowy day in December. Outside the walls of Kells, the forest was covered in a white blanket. The small streams that had raced noisily through the trees during the summer were frozen into silence. The world was very quiet and still, as

if holding its breath, waiting for something to happen. Waiting for it to stop being so very, very cold.

Brendan and Aidan were in the Scriptorium. Even though a wood fire burned in the grate, the Scriptorium was still freezing. It was noon, so the room was very bright. They were working as hard as they could, as the dark days meant that the time they could spend illustrating was very short. They were both bundled up in layers and layers of wool, so that Brendan felt like an onion. When they spoke, their breath was like smoke in the air. They wore woollen gloves on their hands, knitted by Brother Assoua. The woollen fingers had been cut out, so that they could still work, but their finger-tips were purple with the cold.

Aidan blew on his fingertips to warm them up and sighed. 'It will be a hard Christmas this year, with so many mouths to feed and Abbot Cellach pushing so hard to get the wall higher. I wonder will he let you out to join us all for Christmas Day, Brendan? At least to go to the church ...'

Brendan shrugged. 'It doesn't matter. But I wish

he would let me talk to him again. I miss talking to him, even though he used to be cross so much of the time. But Tang says Uncle doesn't take the time to talk at all now; he's working so hard. Everyone is working so hard. Brother Assoua said to me yesterday that the monks are saying my uncle will make them work on Christmas Day itself. Though at least the work keeps them warm. Assoua said he dreams at night of being at home, where the sun shines all the time and the lions go running over the golden plains ...'

'These times are hard on everyone,' said Aidan quietly.

'Yes,' Brendan continued. 'And everyone is really fed up. Brother Friedrich was cracking jokes that it would be easier to be a Northman's slave after the life he has had here during the last few months. That they should employ Uncle Cellach as a slave-driver ...'

Aidan looked pensive. 'That's the problem with wars. Sometimes we become the very thing that we are fighting so hard against.'

They went back to work.

Aidan was mixing inks and Brendan was work-ing on the Chi Ro page. His head bent over it, he went deep into the world of the crystal, the world of tiny detail and bright colour. They were both so caught up in their task that they did not notice that the robin had begun twittering anxiously from the windowsill and Pangur, sleeping at the fire, had raised her head and had begun to miaow a warning.

Abbot Cellach burst into the Scriptorium. His face was deep red with rage, almost the same colour as his cloak. Brother Tang and Brother Assoua were on his heels, closely followed by the rest of the brothers.

'I'm sorry, Brendan, we tried to warn you,' said Assoua dolefully.

'So this is where you are!' said the Abbot angrily. 'I might have guessed you would both disobey my wishes! I went to your cell to get you out, Brendan, and found you gone and the door unlocked. And here you are! The Northmen are nearly upon us, and you have nothing better to do than drawing! And you, Aidan. You are no longer a friend. You have betrayed me. Broken faith with the one who offered you refuge.'

He strode over to where Brendan was and snatched up the Book. Not even looking at what Brendan had done, he angrily tore the page Brendan had been working on and crumpled it up in his hand.

Everyone gasped in horror.

The Abbot himself seemed shocked at what he had done. He stood, looking at the torn fragment clutched in his hand. For a moment, Brendan thought he was really looking at it properly. His face changed, as if the beauty of Brendan's illumination had made him doubt his action.

Tang said eagerly, 'Abbot, let Brendan show you what he has made. It is the most beautiful work I have ever seen ...'

Cellach closed his hand over the piece of vellum and glared at Tang. 'Even you, even you, who I thought wise, have been caught up in this nonsense. All any of you can think about is the Book, the Book, nothing but the Book ... The Book will not protect us when the Northmen come. And they are on their way. That is why I went to get Brendan. A refugee has just come to me in the chapel. He ran many miles in the snow, barefoot and wounded, to come to warn us.'

He paused and looked around; everyone knew that he was finally going to say the words that the monks had dreaded hearing for so long.

'The Northmen are less than a day's march from here. They have plundered the monastery and the village of Kilchoill, just a few miles east of the forest. There is nothing left there now. Some of the villagers fled before the raiders reached the village and are on their way here. Just a handful – that is all that managed to escape. The rest are either dead or captured. Brother Assoua, I want you to go into the forest with the scout and lead them here. You will find him in the Refectory, where they are giving him hot food and warm clothing. Tang, you must call the villagers together. Tell them to come to the Round Tower. We will take refuge there until the Northmen have passed. Be sure to reassure them that the wall will keep us safe. Once the Northmen realise that they cannot get through it or over it, they will pass us by and go on to some other unfortunate place.'

Aidan spoke, 'Cellach, you must listen to me. I have seen the Northman attack, you have not. The wall may hold against them, but I am telling you that the gate will not be strong enough. And it is possible that even the wall, thick and solid as it is, will fall. When they see how strong it is, they will be even more determined to get in. Such a big wall, they will say to themselves, such a big wall must have great treasures behind it. We cannot stay here. We must leave Kells. We must fly before them and leave the monastery to their mercy. Cellach, my old friend, I know that to leave all you have worked so hard for will break your heart. I know that we cannot take the great High Cross or the Round Tower or any of the buildings that you and the brothers have slaved to build. But at least we can save the villagers and ourselves and the Book ...'

'I don't want to hear one more word about the Book! And of course the walls will hold. In the name of the Lord, man, we do not have time for this!'

Abbot Cellach turned. 'Get to work, all of you,' he said sharply to the monks. 'Bring as much food and water and warm clothing as you can into the tower.'

The brothers took flight down the steps.

The Abbot looked at Brendan and Aidan for a long moment. Then he turned his back on them and said, 'You two can stay here. You'll be safe in here with your precious Book!'

The Abbot left the room. Brendan and Aidan could hear the key turn as he locked them in.

They looked at each other. Aidan sighed. 'Oh, Cellach, Cellach, why wouldn't you listen to me?'

He walked to the window and looked out. Far to the east they could see flames reddening the sky. Brendan sniffed the air. He could smell burning on the wind. He looked at Aidan, suddenly realising how old he was. In the light of the window his face was as lined as an old leather book cover.

'Fire, it is always fire they bring with them, destroying our houses and our churches.' Aidan's voice was full of pain. 'We had no stone walls in

Iona,' he continued. 'We thought the sea was enough protection. But it did not protect us, and stone walls would not have made any difference either. There were too many of them. No one could build thick enough walls or tall enough towers to keep us safe, for the evil is always there. Will always come back. It was the summer when they came, a lovely blue day. We could see the boats coming over the horizon, longboats with dragon's heads at the prows. Do you know the strange thing, Brendan? Their boats were beautiful things, graceful and curved and wonderfully made. They have skills of their own, the Northmen, in boat-building and in weapon-making. Their swords are strong. They have designs on the hilts that you would not be ashamed to have made yourself. They are very fond of their weapons. They give them names, you know, the swords. Names like Chopper and Ironmouth, Leg Biter and Blood Drinker and Death Dealer.' He sat down and covered his face with his hands.

'They set the island ablaze. Those that were not burned alive were put to the sword or herded onto the boats like cattle. They tore the gold and silver covers from the sacred books; they knocked over the stone crosses covering the graves of our dead. They laughed as they spat on the holy relics in the church. Oh Brendan, I still see them, hear them sometimes when I sleep at night. We are like animals trapped in a pen here, waiting to be slaughtered ...'

Brendan did not know what to say. He felt sick. Aidan's story had brought back to him the horrible memory of his own worst nightmares.

Aidan looked up and seemed to pull himself together when he saw Brendan's face. 'Ah, Brendan, I should not be talking like this. And you know, as long as I have lived, there is one thing that I have learned. You can never tell exactly what will happen.'

He stood up and joined Brendan at the window. The gates of Kells were being opened to admit a line of bedraggled, freezing figures, struggling through the snow that lay thickly on the ground. Brother Assoua led them. He carried a child in his arms, a little boy wrapped in a cloak stained with blood. There were young and old in the group, but they all moved very, very slowly, with their heads bent low. Their faces were grey. Some of them collapsed on the ground, as soon as they realised that they had reached the monastery, and the brothers and villagers rushed to help them. Brendan looked at Aidan. 'There's so many of them. I wish I could help. Isn't there anything can we do?' he asked.

'We can do nothing but wait and hope,' said Aidan. 'Wait and hope.'

Brendan thought for a moment. 'I hate the thought of us just sitting here waiting for them to come and get us,' he said. 'Do you know what, I think we should get ready to make some more ink.'

Aidan raised his eyebrows. 'Do you really think it is a good time to be illustrating?'

'Not illustrating,' said Brendan. 'But I have an idea that ink might come in useful.'

They worked, and then they waited. But they did not wait for long; for as the sun climbed high over the forest, the smell of burning became stronger and the Northmen came closer and closer to Kells.

11 The sack
of kells

Brendan and Aidan looked out helplessly from the window in the Scriptorium, watching the black crows circling and shrieking in the sky above the forest as the Northmen moved nearer to Kells.

'Why can't we hear them?' asked Brendan.

'We'll hear them soon enough,' said Aidan grimly.

Inside the monastery, there was frenetic activity that verged on panic.

Brendan searched for sight of his uncle. He spotted him, sheltering a small child under his cloak and rushing desperately backwards and forwards, shouting out instructions.

But as he watched, a crow called out and an arrow came racing through the air, shot from one of the Northmen's bows.

'They must be at the gates!' cried Brendan. 'And Uncle has been hit! Oh, why can't I do anything to help!'

The arrow had hit Abbot Cellach in the shoulder, but he continued to run, calling to Tang.

'Brother Tang!' he shouted. 'Open the door of the tower. We have to get as many people as we can inside!'

'There won't be time for everyone to get into the tower,' said Aidan fearfully.

The crowd of villagers and the refugees that had come to the monastery began to rush towards the wooden steps leading to the Round Tower. Brendan could see Tang holding the door open, high up in the wall. As he watched, Brendan realised that the tower could not possibly hold everyone. And some people didn't want to go in. He could see a child, crying, holding on to the last moment to try to convince his father to bring his puppy into the tower with them, and an old woman stubbornly refusing to leave her cow.

There was a crashing noise as the Northmen's

battering ram pounded the wood of the gate. It could only be a matter of moments before they were inside the enclosure. The raiders were no longer silent, but shouting out war whoops and calling encouragement to each other in a strange, guttural language. Arrows came flying over the walls, like a shower of hailstones. There was a pan-icked rush of villagers up the steps. Abbot Cellach was behind them, shouting: 'One at a time! The steps aren't strong enough!'

With that, there was a crash and the steps col-lapsed, bringing dozens of terrified villagers hur-tling to the ground.

'Close the door!' Cellach shouted at Tang, who was watching from the tower doorway. 'Save those who are inside!'

Then with a loud, groaning noise, the gates of Kells burst open and the Northmen spilled into the enclosure, swords and battle-axes raised. There seemed to be hundreds of them. They came swarming through the gate and over the walls like giant insects, looking like the pictures of devils in the Book. Brendan could see them quite clearly:

their fair and dark and red beards under their leather helmets; their short bows and heavy shields; the black markings on their faces. Many of them did not carry swords, but short, brutal-looking battleaxes.

'You were right,' he whispered to Aidan, who was watching beside him. 'There are too many of them. The gate could never have held against them.'

Aidan put his hand on Brendan's shoulder. 'I only wish I could have been wrong. That's the problem with walls. You always have to leave some way in and some way out, unless you want to wall yourself up altogether. Do you know, I think this lot is the same crowd that came to Iona. I recognise those black marks on their faces; it makes them look like badgers. The leader is called Harald Redtooth. Not a nice character. His sword is called Monk Mincer, one of those not very funny Northmen jokes. Move back a bit from the window, Brendan, we don't want them to see us.'

Within a few moments the great stone Cross of

Kells was knocked over, crashing to the ground and breaking as it fell. The raiders had set the thatched roofs of the village ablaze and Brendan covered his ears so as not to hear the panic-stricken noise of the horses and cows trapped in their burning stables and byres. Red blood covered the snow and fire burned up the huts as the screaming animals were rounded up by the Northmen. The old woman who had refused to leave her cow had her arms pulled roughly from its neck and was left to lie in the snow, unconscious. The old and the sick they killed, the younger and stronger were herded together to make the long march through the snow back to the raiders' ships.

'Uncle, did you see Uncle?' Brendan could hear the tremor in his voice as he tried to see through the thick haze of smoke that covered the monastery.

Aidan peered. 'My eyesight isn't what it used to be, but is that him over there?' he said, pointing towards a figure in a dark red cloak.

The Abbot was bent over with pain and the

arrow was still caught in his shoulder. He was limping towards the Scriptorium. He was so close now that Brendan could see his face. Cellach was looking up towards the Scriptorium windows with an expression of agony on his face. His lips were moving and Brendan was sure that he was saying his name.

'He is coming to let us out,' cried Aidan.

'No!' shouted Brendan. He could see what his uncle could not: three Northmen closing in on the Abbot from behind, their swords drawn. Cellach fell to the ground.

'Uncle Cellach!' shouted Brendan, 'No, please don't let this be happening ...'

One of the Northmen came towards the fallen figure and roughly tore something from around his neck. It was the gold lunula the Abbot had always used to fasten his cloak, the sign of his authority in the monastery. The Northman, who Brendan recognised as the one Aidan had pointed out as the chief, Harald Redtooth, pulled his uncle's cloak from him, and wrapped it over his shoulders like a scarf. Then he looked towards the

Scriptorium. His eyes narrowed as he caught sight of Brendan and Aidan at the windows and he grinned, showing black teeth. They pulled back quickly, but it was too late; the chief had called to his comrades to follow him to the Scriptorium door. Aidan and Brendan looked at each other. They could hear the raiders hacking it down.

Now they had to rely on their last desperate plan. It was not a very good plan, but it was the only one they had.

The two of them went into action. They took up vats of half-made ink and while the Northmen raced up the stairs, they added huge quantities of the final ingredient that always set it alight. The ink exploded in a series of loud bangs, creating a thick wall of noxious green smoke.

The raiders, thundering up the stairs, were met with the smoke when they burst into the Scriptorium. The fire and green smoke blinded them as they came in. The ink mixture continued to explode, each time creating a cloud of smoke and an enormous bang. In the confusion, Brendan, Aidan and Pangur managed to escape past the

Northmen through the open door. They raced downstairs, taking nothing with them but the Book and the crystal.

Outside, there was mayhem. Bodies lay everywhere and the Northmen continued to burn and kill. Brendan looked around to where he had seen the Abbot fall. He was still there, stretched on the ground, unmoving. Brendan started to run towards him, but Aidan grabbed him by the arm and whispered fiercely, 'Come on, Brendan, there is no time to delay. You must bring me to the secret passage to the forest. The forest is the only safe place to be now.'

But Brendan pulled away. 'No, we must save him! We must save Uncle Cellach!' He was sobbing as he spoke. 'Look, he's wounded. He might be dead!'

Aidan said desperately, 'Quickly, Brendan, the passage. We have no time at all to lose.'

'We have to save him!' cried Brendan. Tears were streaming down his cheeks.

Aidan knew they could wait no longer. A raider was coming towards them, his blood-stained

battle-axe, raised, ready to attack.

Aidan lifted Brendan up and started to carry him towards the wall. Pangur was leading the way to the gap, going as fast as she could and occasionally looking over her shoulder to make sure that they were following.

'Very well,' said Brendan in a small voice. 'Let me down, Aidan. I'll walk now.'

'Don't walk, *run*,' said Aidan breathlessly. 'We must hope that we will be able to run far enough and fast enough to escape the Northmen, or all your uncle's efforts will have been for nothing!'

The sun was beginning to go down over the trees as they struggled through the snow. It was cold and still, as cold and still as death, thought Brendan. Tears came to his eyes as he thought of his uncle. From somewhere in the shadows, a wolf howled.

Behind them, smoke still rose from the enclosure of the monastery. There was a terrible smell of burning in the air. At least the screams of those who had been caught in the path of the Northmen had died down. Now only the crows called.

Brendan stopped in his tracks.

'I have to go back,' he said to Aidan.

'The Northmen left no one on Iona, and they will leave no one in Kells,' said Aidan sadly. 'You can do nothing for Cellach now. He lived to protect you, and now I must do the same. For Cellach and for the Book.'

They walked on a little and Aidan continued, 'The Northmen will feast in the ruins of the monastery, offering sacrifices to their gods in thanks for a successful raid. That is what they always do. And they always wait to see if those that went into hiding will return. They have their code of conduct. They will not want to leave anything alive in their ...'

Aidan never got to finish his sentence. A dark figure loomed over him and he was lifted into the air and flung to the ground. The satchel was ripped from his hands. Pangur, hissing wildly, flew at the attacker and was batted away, and the Book and the Eye fell from the satchel. The crystal rolled towards Brendan, who quickly slid it behind him so that it was hidden in the roots of a tree.

It was the Chief Northman, the one who had attacked Cellach. Two other Northmen were with him, looking as if they would be more than happy to run Aidan and Brendan through at a word from their leader. The Chief wore the Abbot's lunula, and around his waist were tied the gold and silver treasures of the monastery; jewelled chalices and silver bells and ivory statues. Even from the distance, Brendan could catch the stench of his breath. It reminded him of the smell in Crom Cruach's cave. Redtooth's eyes had lit up when he saw the shining cover of the Book. He muttered something in his strange language: the only word Brendan could make out was what sounded like 'Gold!'

Brendan held his breath while the Northman lifted the Book and turned it over. He seemed to think it was some kind of bag. But nothing fell out. He shook it roughly. Still nothing. Giving a grunt of disgust, he tore the cover roughly from the Book. The pages of vellum fell and scattered on the ground. The Chief, as he turned to go, muttered some words to the two other Northmen. They came closer to Aidan and Brendan and drew out their swords. But just as they raised them, ready for the kill, there was a sound that made them hesitate – the sound of clawed feet running and deep growls. Before the two Northmen could bring down their swords on Aidan and Brendan, they themselves had been brought to the ground.

They turned and twisted, their swords still in their hands, trying to plunge them into the wolves' necks. But the wolves were too quick for them. Teeth fastened on the Northmen's throats. Fighting for their lives, the invaders battled with the wolves, moving away from the clearing and into the wood as they struggled. One especially large wolf raced after the Chief where he had fled through the trees. The rest of the pack surrounded Aidan and Brendan. Brendan began to wonder if they had escaped the Northmen only to be eaten by wild wolves. But then there was a howl from deep in the trees, and, just like the first time Brendan had visited the forest, the wolves raised their heads, as if answering a command. In a moment, they had turned tail and taken flight, disappearing into the darkness, as quickly as they had come.

Brendan took Pangur in his arms and said cautiously to Aidan, who was lying with his eyes closed and breathing heavily, 'Are you hurt?'

Aidan opened his eyes and shook his head. 'I will be grand. I can't believe those wolves didn't attack us, only the Northmen.'

'Me neither,' said Brendan, who had his own ideas as to who had called off the wolf pack. 'At least the Northmen didn't get the crystal or the Book. The cover is gone, but the Book is still there.'

Brendan and Aidan began to gather the pages of the Book. They were scattered all over the clearing. A page was caught up in a gust of wind and blown into the trees, and Brendan ran after it. As he scrabbled in the grass to pick it up, he heard Pangur give a happy miaow, and when he looked up he found he was looking directly into the eyes of a large white wolf. It sat very still, gazing at Brendan. Its eyes were a vivid green. For a moment, there was absolute quiet in the forest. Brendan stared at the wolf and the wolf stared back. Then, the wolf stood up and slowly walked over to where a page of the Book lay on the ground. Very gently, it placed its nose on the page and edged it towards Brendan.

As he looked deep into those green eyes, Brendan knew exactly who the wolf was.

'Aisling,' he whispered. 'It is you, isn't it?'

The corners of the wolf's mouth lifted. Then, with one last look, it turned and raced into the darkness of the trees. The moon came from behind a cloud showing nothing, not even a trail of foot-prints in the snow.

Brendan made his way back to Aidan. They put the scattered pages back into the satchel with the Eye, and, sure that they were safe from further attack as long as they were in the forest, Brendan gathered branches and built a fire. Aidan slept, but although Brendan was exhausted, he sat for a while watching the flames and the moonlight. He found that tears were streaming down his face. He cried for the brothers, for Tang and Assoua and Leonardo, but mostly he cried for his uncle. All his anger with Cellach was gone. The Abbot had only wanted what he thought was best for Brendan and for Kells. He had only wanted to protect him. Brendan remembered his uncle's kindness. He remembered his goodness. He remembered the gentleness that had been hidden by the stern manner. Now he was dead, and Kells was destroyed, and all his uncle's work seemed to have been for nothing.

'Not for nothing,' Brendan whispered fiercely himself. 'I will finish the Book. I will do it for him.'

12 Leaving the Forest

When Brendan opened his eyes the next morning, Aidan was up and about. The old monk was bruised but not badly hurt from his encounter with the Northmen the evening before. Determined to keep their spirits up, he said cheerily, 'Well, lad, the sun is up. Time to be stirring and on the road.'

'Do you think we could look for some food first?' said Brendan. 'I'm starving.'

Aidan said, 'You know, it looks like there is something, or someone, looking after us. It wouldn't happen to be your friend from the forest?'

He nodded to a pile of nuts and berries, and some wizened winter apples. A small clump of snowdrops grew beside it. Brendan bent down and gently touched the flowers.

After they had eaten, Brendan said, 'Where will we go, Aidan? What will we do?'

Aidan sighed. 'I don't think we should try to go to another monastery. Places that were once beacons of learning and peace have become the targets of the Northmen's greed. For the moment anyway, we should find a place where we can do our work in secret. There's more than one way of being a monk, you know. The Abbot's way was one way, and a very good way. But being part of a big group of brothers, and surrounded by all the organisation and the business of Kells is not the only way to serve God. There are many men and women who go down a different path. Saint Kevin, for example, he lived alone in the wilderness and in the wilderness he found God. Though I always think it might have suited him to have lived alone even if he hadn't been a monk and a great saint. He was a bit of a cranky character, you know – he threw a woman in a lake once because she was annoying him.'

For the first time since the Northmen's raid,

Brendan found himself close to smiling.

'You will have to tell me his story, Aidan. But is that what we should do? Live in the wild?'

'We'll see where the road takes us,' said Aidan. 'I think we will know the place we should stay in when we see it. What do you say, Pangur?'

Pangur miaowed happily, and led the way through the trees.

For as long as they travelled through the forest they would find stashes of food left for them every morning, nuts and berries and fruit. The food seemed to give them more strength than ordinary food. This was a very good thing, as the journey was difficult. The snow continued to fall and the nights were icy cold. As they walked, Aidan told Brendan his stories of saints and ancient heroes and magical beings. When he thought Brendan was ready to listen, he also told him about the things the Northmen believed, about their gods and their great sagas. He told Brendan how the Northmen believed that the gods had created the first two humans from two trees. He told him

stories of Baldur the Brave, of the beautiful god-
dess Freya and mischievous god Loki. Brendan
was amazed to hear that the Northmen told stories
about a great serpent who lived deep in the earth
and about a god who sacrificed himself for the
good of his people: Odin the One-Eyed, who had
hung for three days upside down on a tree in order
to find wisdom. Even still, the Northmen thought
that one might meet Odin on the road, a hooded,
one-eyed traveller with two ravens on his shoulder. They were called Hugin and Munin, Thought
and Memory. And as Aidan told his tales, they
walked further and further from Kells. The snow
melted and the wind grew warmer. Spring came
back to the forest.

They travelled south and west, away from the
path of the Northmen. They had many adventures
on their travels. Most of the people they met were
kind to them, and gave them food and shelter. All
of them wanted to hear the story of how they had
escaped from the Northmen.

Finally, one day, as they walked through mist

and rain up a mountain that seemed never ending, Aidan suddenly grabbed Brendan's arm and forced him to come to an abrupt standstill. The mist slowly cleared and they found themselves standing at the very edge of a rocky cliff. The path ahead of them ended in air, and they were looking down into the most beautiful green valley, bounded on the far side by the arc of a rainbow. A waterfall fell down from the heights of the hills to the valley floor, and formed a lake at the bottom. From the lake flowed a curving silver river. On the eastern edge of this river there grew a small oak wood. To the south and west, the valley opened out. And there, where the land sloped down towards the water's edge, was the sea. The river flowed into the bay just where a curve of golden beach met the blue water. The sun was beginning to go down over the water and Brendan thought he had never seen anything so beautiful as the light dancing on the waves.

He looked at Aidan and Aidan looked at him. Brendan nodded. 'It's here, isn't it?' he said.

The three of them made their way slowly and

carefully into the valley, and slept that night in the shelter of the oak wood.

The next day Brendan wanted to start gathering berries for ink.

Aidan said, 'No, first things first. We have to build a proper shelter. A bothy in the trees is all very well for the summer, but the winter will be back soon and the wind and the rain will come at us from the west. We have to be prepared for that. We have to build well. And as your uncle knew, the best buildings are made of stone.'

Brendan groaned. 'And you are beginning to sound like him. I thought that after I left Kells I would never, ever again have to drag stones around.'

Aidan laughed. 'Never say never. Ah, come on, lad. It won't take that long; we are just going to build the basics. Two little cells, that's all we need.'

So through the summer days they worked, and built two small stone huts to Aidan's design. They were round and windowless, and reminded Brendan of the beehives he had looked after in

Kells. They also planted vegetables and herbs, and they gathered berries and made new ink. They searched for fallen feathers in the forest, and from these they made pens. And by the time autumn came, Brendan was able to begin work on the Book. While he worked, Aidan talked to him, advised him, and told him more stories. The valley was very quiet. Sometimes a hunter or a fisherman would come upon them, and they would feed their visitor and ask for news of the outside world.

One day a wild-looking man with a very hairy face arrived in the valley and asked Aidan to hear his confession. Aidan was very quiet and serious after their conversation. Brendan realised why when he saw the strange man baying at the moon that night.

'He's a werewolf, isn't he?' he whispered to Aidan.

Aidan nodded. 'He is. He's a Kilkenny man, and they are desperately prone to it. But he is a good man. You know St Ronan was a werewolf too, or at least his wife said he was. She used to complain that she could never get a decent night's sleep because of the racket he made when the moon was full.'

Sometimes they themselves would make a journey out of their forest in the valley and visit one of the tiny villages nearby. They were always made welcome. Aidan became famous as a storyteller and the children, especially, loved to hear his tales.

They built a currach and would fish on the lake or out to sea. On clear, warm evenings they would go to the cliffs, at the edge of the coast, and look to the west as the sun set over the ocean. They often went walking on the long beaches along the shore, following the line at the edge of the water, where the sand met the sea and the sun made everything shine silver and gold. Aidan would smile into the setting sun and tell Brendan of his dreams of going further west.

'Like your namesake, Brendan, the Great Navigator. Did I ever tell you the story of how he landed on a whale and thought it was an island? Ah, I did. I must have told you every story I know by now. But, you know, no one really knows what is out there, out to the west. You might reach the edge of the world and fall off, into God knows what. It would be a marvellous thing to see the place where the sun goes down.'

He paused. 'Brendan, I have a favour to ask you. When I go, and you know I will have to go sooner or later, I want you to put me into a boat and send me westwards, into the setting sun.'

'You're not going anywhere,' Brendan would say. 'You are staying here with me and Pangur.'

'Ah Brendan, don't be upset that I'm talking to you like this. The line between life and death is a narrow one, you know. It is no more constant than that line where the tide meets the sand.'

All through this time, Brendan worked on illustrating the Book. He tried to put everything he knew into it. Everything he had felt in his heart and thought with his head. The sounds and smells of the forest; the feeling of the green moss on the tree under his hand. And he put in all those he had loved.

He put in Aisling, now as a white-haired angel, now as a wolf, now as a white bird with a human face, now as a twisting of pale flowers in a margin. He put in the Abbot, with his sad stern face and his tall figure. Cellach had a Book in his hand, open, finally taking the time to look inside. He put in each of the lost brothers: Leonardo, Assoua, Friedrich and Jacques. They peered out at him from under the tall letters and bands of colour. He put in Assoua's lions, although he found he could not remember the description all that well, and when he looked at what he had drawn, he was not sure it was exactly right. He put in the otter he had seen in the forest, with the fish in its mouth; he put in the eagles he had seen flying over the high mountains they had crossed on their way to their valley. He put in the shy deer and the clever foxes; the mice that had kept him company in his cell and the robin that had looked on as he learned to draw. He put in the moths he had seen flitting in the light between the trees. He even put in the monster, Crom Dubh. It became a green serpent that wriggled and curled through the borders, swallowing its own tail. He put in the spiral path in the forest, the path that had led him to knowledge and

wisdom. And again and again, he drew the tree of life. Every time he drew it, it was different and more wonderful, as if the drawings themselves were growing like trees, as he himself had grown. And when Pangur played with her kittens, he put them in too. He drew them as they crawled over her back and played tag under her legs.

Pangur never seemed to get any older. But the years passed and Brendan grew up, until he was no longer a boy but a young man. And Aidan grew older too, until he became very old and very tired, and one spring morning he did not wake up. Brendan found him in his bed in his little cell, a smile on his face, and Pangur curled at his feet.

13 the book
of kells

After he had prayed over him, Brendan took Aidan's body from his cell and made a bier of green branches. With the help of those who had come to mourn with him, he carried him to the coast. There he placed him in the currach that he and Aidan had built to go fishing in the sea. He pointed the prow westwards and sent it out with the tide into the light of the setting sun. He felt the tears fall as he watched the tiny boat go further and further away from him.

But even as Aidan's body was pulled away from him, Brendan felt a presence beside him. He looked towards the west and the light of the evening sun dazzled his eyes, but he thought he could see a familiar figure standing at his side. He was holding something out to Brendan. It was the Book.

He heard Aidan's voice on the wind:

'The Book was never meant to be hidden away behind walls, locked away from the world that inspired its creation. Brendan, you must take the Book to the people, so that they may have hope. Let it light the way in these dark days.'

And then the wind rose, and the sun was lost behind the line of the ocean, and the shadowy figure was gone.

Brendan was lonely without Aidan's company. Sitting in his cell, he thought of Aidan's words and wondered where he should bring the Book. The Northmen still raided the monasteries and villages, although not as wildly as they had done during the years before. They had even begun to settle down in some places, planting crops in the soil and marrying and trading with the Irish. But where would the Book be safe from their wilder cousins, who still landed quietly in the night and pillaged the holy places? He thought of Clonmacnoise and Cashel and Glendalough, all of them great monasteries with master illuminators who would look after the Book well. But in the end, he realised that there was only one place for the Book to go. That there was only one place where he himself wanted to go to. He gathered his few possessions into the same leather satchel that held the Book long years before. He looked at Pangur as she dozed by the fire, with one eye open, watching his every move.

'I'm sorry, old cat,' he said. 'You are too old for this journey. Stay here with your children and grandchildren. The villagers will look after you.' Pangur did not even miaow her protest. She simply jumped onto his shoulders and dug in her claws, determined as always not to be left behind.

After many weeks travelling, they came at last to the edge of the great forest. Brendan looked at it in dismay. It was a tangle of undergrowth, of branches and furze and nettles and thorns.

'I'll never be able to find my way through this,' he said to Pangur.

Pangur did not look too worried, but merely lay down under a convenient oak tree and closed her eyes. And so Brendan, who had no better ideas as regards what to do next, did the same.

Brendan woke up. While they had slept, the moon had risen and was shining brightly. The light seemed to show a path through the thickety undergrowth. He was sure that the path had not been there when he went to sleep. Brendan thought he heard a child's laughter. He shook his head slightly, trying to clear his mind. Was he dreaming? Was this his imagination? Along the path grew a drift of snowdrops. And on the path, so far away that Brendan could not be altogether sure of what he saw, there seemed to be the figure of a girl with long white hair. He started up, hardly daring to believe his eyes. But as he watched, the figure grew taller. It was no longer a child but a beautiful white-haired woman. He blinked, trying to see more clearly, and now it had changed again, changed into an old, old woman, stooping low over the flowers. All of this hap-pened within seconds.

'Aisling,' he tried to say, 'it is you, isn't it? Won't

you talk to me? Won't you let me see you and hear you the way you did before?'

But it seemed as if his voice was no longer working, for no words came out. There was only silence and stillness in the forest. This can't be real, he thought to himself. This can't be happening.

Then a further change came upon the figure. It was no longer human. A white wolf stood before him, watching him, its eyes bright green, shining in the moonlight. Brendan drew back, holding his breath in wonder. Aisling had indeed come to lead him through the forest.

'Aisling,' he said again, and now he knew he was awake because he could hear his voice in the darkness. 'Can't you speak to me?'

But the white wolf did nothing but incline her head in the direction she wanted Brendan to follow. Brendan gathered Pangur up and followed her lead deep into the dark wood.

A storm was breaking over Kells. Black clouds raced across the sky and the wind howled through the broken stones and lashed the ivy against the crumbling walls. Rain came down in sheets and lightning flashed, illuminating the frail figure that stood at the window of the Round Tower, looking out into the darkness. The great Abbey of Kells now housed only a handful of monks and villagers. The stones that had been piled up, one on top of the other, with so much thought and with so much labour by the Abbot and the brothers, had almost all fallen to the ground. The gate hung loose on its hinges, and vines and green brambles covered the walls. The forest had reclaimed Kells. Indeed, it was hard to tell where the forest ended and the monastery began.

But there were still some signs of life. Smoke rose from the huts that circled the chapel, now rebuilt as a smaller but solid little building. There were vegetable plots scattered around the enclosure; cattle and sheep lowed in the pens, and pigs grunted as they scrabbled in the mud. A goose flew by, with a small boy in pursuit, determined to catch it so it could be put inside, safe from the storm. The bird stopped for a moment on the broken cross, then flew on towards the roofless

Scriptorium. Doves nested there, and during the day they flew in and out, carrying food for their young from the forest. But tonight the doves were huddled in their nests.

Brother Tang, older now and even wiser, went to the window and placed his hand gently on the shoulder of the man who stood there.

'Please rest now, Abbot,' he said.

'How can I rest when I think of what we have lost? Of our most precious treasure?' asked the Abbot. But he finally allowed Tang to lead him back to bed. There he tossed feverishly, still unable to sleep. Tang looked at him anxiously. He knew that Abbot Cellach would not be much longer in the world, and he wished that his old friend could find some peace before he left them.

'There is no time,' said the Abbot feebly. 'Oh, I don't want to die, Tang. Not yet. I could go happily if only I knew I had done some good in the world. But all my life, everything I tried to do has been a failure. I could not save my brothers nor my people. I could not save Brendan. I could not save the Book. Oh, if only Brendan could have been saved!'

'Do not fret yourself,' said Tang softly. 'Try to rest.'

But the Abbot sighed deeply and said, his voice fading to a whisper. 'We are lost.'

A hooded figure moved forward out of the shadows at the top of the stairs. Tang looked up, aware that someone had entered the tower.

The Abbot drew back in terror. 'Angel of darkness!' he called. 'Not yet! Do not take me yet! I need more time!'

The figure moved forward.

'Oh, let it not be the angel of death!' said Cellach again. 'Or some fairy creature come in from the forest!'

With a start of joyful recognition, Tang moved towards the cloaked figure with the small white cat at its side. The stranger put his finger to his lips, motioning Tang to stay silent. Then he moved forward towards the bed.

'You always said there was no such thing as fairies, Uncle,' said Brendan, throwing back his rain-soaked hood and laughing. The moon came from behind a cloud as he clasped his uncle's hands in his.

'Holy God and all his angels!' said Brother Tang.

But the Abbot could say nothing. His mouth moved but no words came out. He held onto Brendan's hands as if he would never let them go. Finally, he found his voice. 'Brendan!' he said. 'It is a dream.'

'This is no dream, Uncle,' said Brendan. He himself was finding it hard to believe that his uncle had not been killed; that he and Tang had survived and stayed in the Abbey, keeping a light burning in Kells through all the long years since the Northmen's raid.

'My boy!' Cellach whispered. 'You survived! And have grown up so tall. How did you manage it?'

'How did I manage to grow up?' Brendan laughed again. 'I didn't have to do much, it just happened!'

But now Abbot Cellach was moving restlessly again, his memories of the raid bringing back the guilt that had tormented him for many years.

'So many dead ... so many innocent lives lost. All of it my fault.'

'Please, Uncle,' said Brendan, 'Don't distress yourself.'

'You don't understand,' said the Abbot. 'You were right. About Kells. About Aidan. About the Book. I shouldn't have acted as I did.'

He opened his hand and showed Brendan what he held in it.

'This is all I have left,' he said. 'This is the only comfort I have in the world.'

Brendan looked closely and saw that what he held was the tiny piece of vellum which Brendan had been illustrating just before the Northmen raided. The piece of the Book that his uncle, in his anger, had tried to destroy. Cellach had kept it, treasured it as a memory of Brendan and as a small piece of beauty, ever since that dreadful time.

Brendan reached into his satchel, but as he did so, Tang, unable to contain himself any longer, asked excitedly, 'But Brendan, how did you escape the Northmen? We were sure that you and Aidan had been killed or captured!'

So Brendan told them the story of how Aidan and himself had managed to escape from Kells through the secret entrance. Then he asked what had happened in the Abbey after they had made their escape.

It was Tang who told the tale, for his uncle had been very ill for a long time after having been wounded by the raiders. Tang began:

'It was the strangest of things, the way it happened, the way they left. I watched everything from the Round Tower. Those of us inside were safe from the raiders, as we could defend the door. They were still at their burning and destroying when some kind of fight broke out. A tall one with a black beard began to shout. It looked like he wanted something that the leader, the red-haired one, had. I couldn't see what it was, but we thought afterwards that it must have been the lunula from the Abbot's cloak. Anyway, they argued and argued and shouted at each other and then the axes came out. Then one of them pointed at something, and I saw, perched on the window-sill of the Scriptorium, a white bird. I have never seen a bird like it. It was a big one, and it cawed like a raven.

I could hear the Northmen getting anxious. I heard some of them mention Odin, and it seemed as if they had started to think that this place held bad luck for them. In any case, they decided not to wait around any longer. I don't know if they went into the forest or back to their ships. They took most of the villagers and the monks with them – or at least those that were left alive – but they didn't go near the Abbot, because they thought he was dead.

When I was sure they were gone, I climbed down from the tower and went over to Abbot Cellach. I could hardly believe it when I found he was still breathing. Those of us that were left nursed him, until he woke up ...'

Tang paused.

'That was nearly the hardest part, Brendan. Because of course, the first thing he did was ask after you. And I had to tell him that I thought the Northmen had taken you and Aidan. He nearly didn't want to come back to us then, from the dark place he was in. But I reminded him that he had to lead the few of us that were left in Kells. That he was the Abbot of Kells and he still had his duty to do. After that – well, after that – there were many long days of re-building and replanting. It's hard to do such work the first time, but it's harder still the second time, when all the work you did at the beginning has been destroyed. But there were small things that gave us hope, small lights in the darkness. And now that you have returned we can see that our hope was justified.'

'Yes,' interrupted Cellach. 'Because you and Aidan survived. But if only I had listened to Aidan!'

Brendan said, 'Brother Aidan never did pay you much heed, Uncle.'

Cellach looked surprised for a moment, and then laughed. 'I suppose he didn't,' he said.

As they spoke, the night ended and the storm quietened over Kells. The room in the tower was gradually filled with the light of a new day.

Brendan smiled at his uncle. He reached into his satchel as he said, 'Brother Aidan lived to see his work passed on and completed.'

And he handed Cellach the Book.

For a moment, Cellach looked into Brendan's eyes, as if afraid to believe what was in front of him.

'Go on,' said Brendan. 'Look.'

Abbot Cellach slowly opened the Book. His hands turned page after page, as tears of joy rolled down his cheeks.

'So beautiful,' he whispered, 'So beautiful.'

And then, when he came to the Chi Ro page, he could go no further, dazzled by the light and caught as he was in the intricate web of colour and form, the jewelled patterns that shone and sparkled and seemed to fill the whole room with brightness. Finally he said, 'The Book of Iona.'

'The Book of Kells?' said Brendan, a question in his voice.

And his uncle repeated after him, his voice full of wonder, 'The Book of Kells.'

The Chi Ro page of the Book of Kells

the book of kells

The Book of Kells is a precious book of the Christian gospels, created over 1,200 years ago, around AD800. This type of book is known as an illuminated manuscript.

The book was made in a monastery. We do not know the names of the monks who wrote and illustrated the book, but more than one person worked on the 680 pages.

The monasteries of Iona and Kells

A monastery was made up of a small group of people who felt that God wanted them to do special work. These people were called monks.

Some monasteries had a special writing room, called a scriptorium, where the monks could do their wonderful work. Two monasteries are connected to the Book of Kells: the monastery at Iona, a small windswept island off the west coast of Scotland and the monastery at Kells, in County Meath in Ireland. Some people believe the book was begun on Iona, perhaps even when St Columba (also called Columcille) was still there. Two hundred years after the death of St Columba, the island of Iona was invaded by the Vikings (called the Northmen in the novel) who came across the sea from Norway to rob and destroy the monastery. The abbot escaped and made his way to Kells in Ireland.

the vikings

The Vikings were fighters and pagans from Scandinavia. Their longboats sailed across the ocean and rowed up the rivers to launch surprise attacks on monasteries and other settlements. For many years the Vikings kept up their hit-and-run attacks on Ireland and then they began to set up towns such as Dublin, Wexford and Cork.

how the book of kells was made

The Book of Kells was written on vellum (calfskin). It took about 150 calves to supply the pages for the manuscript. The scribes wrote with a pen made out of reed or a quill, sometimes a goose feather. Some of the inks were made from the juices of plants, berries, leaves and roots; others were made from metals and minerals: the red from red lead, the yellow, or gold, from orpiment (a mineral), some of the green from copper and the blue from the precious stone *lapis lazuli*.

The Book of Kells can be seen today in Trinity College, Dublin. It remains one of Ireland's most visited treasures.

*To find out more, you can read **Exploring The Book of Kells** by George Otto Sims and **The Vikings in Ireland** by Morgan Llywelyn. Both books available from www.obrien.ie.*

Brendan's story is also available
for younger children
as a beautiful full-colour
picture book

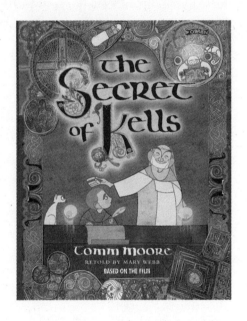

From the animated film
by the Cartoon Saloon